The Gentleman's Betrothal

A Second Chance Historical Romance

Kerri Kastle

Kerri Kastle

Copyright © 2025 by Kerri Kastle

All rights reserved.

No portion of this book may be reproduced in any form without written permission from the publisher or author, except as permitted by U.S. copyright law.

Contents

1. Chapter One — 1
2. Chapter Two — 10
3. Chapter Three — 19
4. Chapter Four — 30
5. Chapter Five — 41
6. Chapter Six — 51
7. Chapter Seven — 62
8. Chapter Eight — 74
9. Chapter Nine — 86
10. Chapter Ten — 95
11. Chapter Eleven — 104
12. Chapter Twelve — 114
13. Chapter Thirteen — 123
14. Chapter Fourteen — 133

15.	Chapter Fifteen	142
16.	Chapter Sixteen	153
17.	Chapter Seventeen	163
18.	Chapter Eighteen	174
19.	Chapter Nineteen	186
20.	Chapter Twenty	197
21.	Chapter Twenty-One	202
	Epilogue	209

Chapter One

"It appears your guests have arrived," Lady Theodora Foxworth said offhandedly, lounging in a cushioned sofa in the spacious drawing room. A fashionable coach with an embedded family crest stopped in clear view of the giant window, the first in a line of others soon to come.

"You mean *our* guests," Alexander, the Earl of Radnor, corrected smoothly with a sharp raise of his dark eyebrows. "You promised you would be in attendance at the hunting party this year."

Dora frowned. "And I intend to heed that promise until the end of the week."

"Only one week? Stay till the end of the month at least," Alex prompted, laying the newspaper he'd been reading aside. His tone was mild and unassuming, but anyone who knew him well could sense the undertone of command in his tone.

"I need to return to London without fail," Dora insisted, turning around fully to give him a withering glare.

"*Why* do you have to?"

"My thoughts and inclinations are none of your business," Dora retorted, a slow blush making its way across her pale face. "I'm returning to London soon, and you can't stop me!"

A sulky silence fell in the room, but it was soon broken by Alex. "I *can* stop you," he responded calmly. "I have the legal power and influence to do so, but I won't. You are my sister after all, and there are no advantages to being a tyrant."

"Such arrogance!"

"Enough of that, you two," Liana interrupted softly, halting the argument between her older siblings. She set an unfinished strip of knitting down as a teasing smile played on her lips. "If anyone saw you two bickering, they'd be amused beyond measure, and the Foxworths would lose their long-standing reputation for being even-tempered aristocrats."

Alex pondered her statement with an amused look. "Haven't we already? Given Dora's temper, it's surprising that anyone accords us any respect."

"I'm only guilty of being expressive in a world that disapproves of such frankness, dear brother," Dora defended. "You, on the other hand, are domineering, but your status as a man makes it so that no one ever criticizes you for it."

"You each have dispositions that reveal themselves in various manners," Liana said placatingly. "Neither is more correct than the other."

Dora laughed, her irritation forgotten. "Always the mediator, sweet little sister. Where would we be without you?"

"Cooperating, I hope?" Liana replied with optimism.

"How fanciful," Alex remarked, folding the newspaper. "We're Foxworths, descendants of a lengthy list of headstrong aristocrats. It is characteristic of us.

"In any case," Dora continued, settling more comfortably in her seat. "*If* I do decide to remain in Suffolk for more than a week, I may as well take an interest in this year's party. Who, might I ask, have you invited?"

In the usual manner of lords of country estates, Alex hosted annual social events ranging from simple house parties for friends and family to hunting parties that went on for weeks and had other peers, wealthy businessmen, and political leaders in attendance. In elite London circles and neighboring environs, it was considered a privilege to be invited by the Earl of Radnor to Ravenmoore Estate, located in the northern part of Suffolk and renowned for its vast land holdings measuring nearly three thousand acres with ample forests and copious lakes.

Guests from various parts of the country and abroad turned up with hopes of entertainment, some bearing ambitions of finding willing partners for their business plans. When the month ended, they all departed with the undeniable certainty of having enjoyed an excellent summer. If Liana didn't know better, she would think the yearly events didn't matter to Alex one way or the other, considering he was typically so formal and controlled in speech and behavior. But one only had to notice the bright glint that appeared in his eyes at the start of September, and the knowledge that Alex enjoyed the advantages of his status would become apparent.

Alex was a proud man with a "colossal confidence that overcame every obstacle, his fierce ambition matched adequately by his kindness to all, strangers included, and an unparalleled devotion to the only living members of his immediate family—his sisters. Dora's personality reminded Liana of their late father's. She was blunt and possessed a fiery temperament, with a propensity to argue about ideas stemming from strongly held opinions. And while she'd earned her share of opposition, her sharp wit was respected and even admired in certain intellectual London groups.

In comparison, Liana was severely ordinary and, were it not for her Foxworth heritage, would likely be dismissed at first glance by a stranger walking into the room. Despite just turning twenty-three, she had more regrets than most people did at that age, and they were presumably enough to haunt her for the rest of her life.

By some unfavorable miracle, the ardent blood that spurred her ancestors to win wars and attain glory had diminished in her. And while Foxworths were distinguished by their obsidian hair and outstanding blue eyes, her sepia brown locks and warm amber eyes only seemed to set her apart further.

Pulled from her thoughts by her brother's voice as he began to speak, Liana transferred her knitting to a nearby footstool to indicate she was listening.

"The Beaumonts are coming, and so are the Garveys," Alex responded.

"How unsurprising," Dora said drily. "It would be near scandalous to host events without extending invites to our dearest cousins."

"Not all of them. Last year, John Garvey and his friend Finn Haskett were caught sneaking into the forest to hunt grey foxes for their pelts. They did this despite warnings not to because the foxes were newly imported and required time to adapt to their new surroundings."

Dora shook her head, untamed curls of springy raven hair mirroring her movement. "What rogues. I hope you punished them adequately."

"Contrary to certain opinions, I'm not a tyrant," Alex said with a mocking smile. "But I did take the liberty of excluding our cousin and his friend from this year's invitation list."

"Aunt Theresa will not be pleased with your decision," Liana said, dreading her aunt's frosty attitude and the way it seemed to hover like a vengeful ghoul.

Alex shrugged. "I'll handle her."

"Who else is coming?" Dora asked, leaning forward in interest.

"The St. Clairs, the Duke of Drummond, a few French barons." He went on to share more names, impressively listing them from memory.

Each member of the Foxworths had a specific talent. Alex had an excellent memory and was good with numbers, and Dora was a skilled artist whose poignant paintings were displayed in a handful of galleries. Liana's affinity for music had led her to master over a dozen musical instruments. Of them all, she best liked the dulcimer. She didn't like playing for an audience and declined to do so despite being regularly urged to. Other than her siblings, the only other person she had ever played the dulcimer for ... was him.

"By Davis, do you mean Colonel Davis, the decorated war hero?" Liana asked in an attempt to distract herself from thoughts arising from the past.

Her brother nodded. "The one and only."

"The ladies would no doubt trip over their gowns fawning for him," Dora said with amusement. "Is that all?"

Alex shot her a look of suspicion. "Were you expecting anyone else?"

"I was only being curious!"

"I find it convenient that the subject of invitees has garnered so much interest from you."

An inexplicable pink flush rose over Dora's face again. Looking affronted, she folded her arms and huffed loudly. "I shall not be made to feel guilty for asking innocent questions."

Alex's icy blue eyes found Liana, settling on her with an inscrutable gaze. "The final name will undoubtedly come as a surprise to you, but I promise his presence isn't ill-intentioned."

Liana felt her breath cease for what seemed like an endless moment. There weren't many people whose sudden appearances could potentially create friction in her life. If Alex was exerting himself to reassure her, that could only mean one thing.

"I have invited Gregory Holt to be a part of the festivities," Alex revealed, observing her carefully for a reaction. "I didn't get an affirmative reply from him until today. Otherwise, I would have shared the news much earlier. His letter had likely been delayed due to errors in the post."

Liana's stomach churned uneasily, ushering in a wave of nausea. She felt a combination of shock and nervousness, accompanied by the rapid pace of her heart. Gregory Holt. The man who had shown her what pure love felt like. The man whose heart she had broken, a sheen of hurt and anger vividly clear in those sea-green eyes.

"Take deep breaths," Dora urged, placing a calming hand on her shoulder.

Liana complied, inhaling and exhaling as the tightness in her chest eased moderately. "I'm alright," she murmured in a quivering voice.

"Why would you invite him?" Dora asked Alex in disbelief.

"He's here to discuss an urgent matter that cannot be delayed until my return to London. He has assured me that this will be a professional visit and there will be no sentimental exchanges between himself and Liana," Alex explained, his gaze softening. "He has agreed to leave the past behind. In the instance that our agreement is breached, I shall escort him off the estate myself."

Dora remained unconvinced. "Mr. Holt is one of your closest friends. Considering you've already invited him here, I'm not confident you'll take necessary measures if need be."

"Don't doubt my intentions, Dora," Alex replied in a voice as hard as steel. "I have done nothing to earn your skepticism. Moreover, Liana is my sister, and I care for her as much as you do."

Dora had the grace to look chastened. "I know, Alex. I'm just worried."

Alex didn't appear to share the same sentiment. "It's been four years since the affair with Gregory. Frankly, it's high time everyone moved beyond it."

"You're right," Liana spoke up, managing to get the words out despite a surge of dizziness. "Focusing on that won't serve any good."

Her brother frowned. "That isn't what I meant. You're allowed to feel these emotions. They're yours, after all."

"It's awfully ill-mannered to center my feelings in this when I'm the one who ended our engagement."

Alex gave her a kind smile. "Feelings are not always governed by logic, yet they hold their own sway."

Gregory had also said something to that effect four years ago, on the day after his arrival at Ravenmoore Estate. Liana had been captivated by him at first sight, unable to keep her eyes from straying to the tall, dark-haired stranger with thoughtful viridian eyes. Having shared many classes with Alex at Cambridge, the two men had cultivated an easy friendship made obvious by their shared jokes and effortless banter.

Spurred by a stint of bravery, she'd invited Gregory to watch her play the pianoforte. He had marveled at her talent, showering her with heartfelt compliments till she was a stammering, blushing mess. He then confessed that he'd earlier resolved to admire her from afar, but he could no longer do so due to his growing feelings, which remained persistent even though his reason deemed the entire process too impulsive and rapid.

From that point on, they had eased into an afternoon routine of Liana playing the dulcimer or another musical instrument while Gregory paid rapt attention and expressed his appreciation for the music.

With her parents dead and no one to care for her except her older siblings, Liana had contended with the harsh likelihood of being overlooked or dismissed for the rest of her life. Gregory's presence had dispelled that notion. He committed her favorite poems to memory and wrote her letters every day, hand-delivered to the tiny box outside her bed chamber. He could listen to her talk for hours without requiring a break, his jokes amused her so intensely that her laughter became gasps, and he doted on her tirelessly as though she were a revered goddess walking the earth.

She hadn't minded that Gregory's brother, Russell, was being accused in a widely discussed murder case that drew the attention of everyone in the country. Or that being associated with Gregory could be scandalous and, as such, affect her family's social standing. He was a man who loved her with unreserved devotion, and that was what mattered most.

By the third month of their resplendent relationship, Gregory had proposed and wedding preparations had begun. It had seemed then that their lives together would continue unimpacted in a sweet, blissful journey. Looking back now, Liana could see how much was ruined due to her naivety. In place of honesty, she'd chosen deception. And as a result, there were many irreparable consequences.

"Liana?" Dora called, concern etched on her features.

"I'm alright," Liana repeated, rising from her seat. "I just need some time alone."

"I'll leave you to it—but promise me you'll maintain your composure when you see him. Whatever you do, do not apologize or cry. It's of no use and will only worsen matters."

"I promise," Liana replied, growing pools of anxiety rippling within her as she exited the room.

Chapter Two

Liana left the manor, taking the back entrance to avoid the deluge of arriving guests. She waded through the dense thicket of the nearby forest, slowing as she reached a section of the Bracken Lake, where diversely colored lilies and peonies grew on the sandy shorefront.

She used to come here with Gregory every week. He would roast freshly caught carp over a fire, seasoned generously the way she liked it, and serve it alongside a spread of dishes prepared by the manor's cook.

It was on one such day that Gregory had shared that his brother Russell, whom he believed innocent, required his help in transferring a business cargo to Brazil. The trip would take months to complete, but the probable monetary gains were great. She'd seen in his eyes a desire to help his brother by leaving England, but it was clear he was hesitant for her sake.

It had occurred to Liana that if he stayed for her, passing up the opportunity to revive his family's dwindled fortune, there was a likelihood that he would later resent that decision. Although it nearly sawed her heart apart to do so, Liana had ended their engagement. Except, instead of telling the truth, she'd told him that, due to his reputation and parentage, he wasn't fit to be her husband and never would be.

The words had tasted raw and untrue in her mouth, but they achieved the desired effect. Gregory had departed the estate shortly after, and Liana subsequently collapsed onto the floor of her bedroom in a fit of tears and misery.

Four years had passed since that incident. Gregory never returned to Ravenmoore Estate, and their paths didn't cross in London. According to what she heard, his trip to Brazil had proven extremely successful. He'd returned with a substantial payment, a quarter of which he used in to employ a capable investigator of crimes. named Jack Cole, who initiated a new inquiry into Russell Holt's murder case. Russell was pronounced innocent due to new evidence, and the two brothers dedicated themselves afterwards to restoring the estate their father, a kind viscount, had left behind.

Gregory may now consider her akin to a cruel shrew, but she would try to interact with him without feeding into ill feelings. Filled with confidence from the new decision, she turned to leave the lake.

A sudden snap echoed beneath her. She glanced down to find her foot stuck in an animal trap. The feeling was more numb than painful, but she refrained from trying to remove her feet to avoid making matters worse.

The sound of footsteps alerted Liana to someone approaching. As she raised her head to look, a singular name echoed repeatedly in her mind.

Gregory.

He was a tall man with broad shoulders that fit snugly in high-quality clothes and sun-kissed skin from spending time outdoors. His hair was as curly as she remembered, the thick layers cut in a short, ruffled style. And his lush green eyes, which once bore great passion for her, now flickered impassively toward her.

"What are you doing?" The sharp edge in his voice swept over her in a chilling tone.

She opened her mouth wordlessly a couple of times like a fish cast upon the shore before finding her voice. "I wasn't watching where I was walking, and I got caught in this," she explained, pointing at the trap while her face simultaneously reddened in embarrassment.

Even after four years, she was still the same woman, so often receiving help or pity from others. Only this time, Gregory no longer seemed pleased with the prospect of spending more time than necessary in her presence.

"It would be best not to squirm," he instructed as he approached. The passing years had been more than kind to him, refining the contours of his face into an advanced form of flawless handsomeness. She couldn't stop herself from staring at him, wondering what new details and incidents he had experienced since.

When he crouched before her, she had to remind herself to breathe. He pried the trap apart effortlessly, creating an opening, and lifted her foot carefully away from the sharp edges.

"The trap was faulty, and that's the only reason why you weren't seriously injured," he said, rising to his feet. "Can you walk?"

Liana took a few tentative steps before nodding. "Thank you for helping me."

Wordlessly, he picked up the animal trap and tossed it behind some shrubs before turning to leave.

"Wait," she whispered, giving in to the persistent urge to keep him around for longer.

His movements halted. "What for?"

"I want to know how you've been," Liana responded. "I ... I am aware of how foolish this sounds, given the shared history between us."

Gregory turned fully and regarded her with cold eyes. "Shared history? That's one way to describe it."

"Should I have termed it otherwise?" She found herself asking. The pit of nervousness inside her grew as she stood trapped within the confines of his heavy gaze.

"On second thought, I think history is quite an apt description," he continued reflectively. "Insignificant histories ought to be left in the past."

Calling out to him had been a foolish, rash act. What had she expected? That he would greet her with a friendly smile and joyfully recount his best moments in England and abroad?

"You'll be present in Suffolk for the following weeks," Liana began, discomfited by the strained air between them. "I ... I think it would be best to spend them without awkward feelings."

"That is something we can both agree on," Gregory replied. "I'm here solely on business motives, and I promised your brother I wouldn't complicate matters."

"I won't venture to induce conflict," Liana murmured. "Not deliberately, that is."

"That would be well appreciated."

Liana inhaled shakily. There were more thoughts she longed to express, but the fear of another cold reaction gave her pause. Perhaps it was best to postpone speaking until a later time. *Or not*, Liana thought. After years of no communication, filling the silences was the least she could do.

"I'm sorry for everything," she said, twisting her fingers. "I shouldn't have implied that you were insignificant or unworthy of me."

The day Gregory left the estate had been the most agonizing event in her life. For several weeks afterwards, she had fallen asleep each night with a teary face and an apology on her lips. She could hardly bear to imagine how hurtful it had felt for him, too, heartbroken and reeling from the sudden betrayal.

"You were correct at the time," Gregory responded calmly. "I was foolish to believe that a genuine romance could exist between a man with a disgraced family name and a spoiled heiress who had everything handed to her on a plate."

Like a solidly wedged rock, he was clearly unwilling to grant her the slightest hint of absolution. Not that Liana could blame him. She had, after all, hurt him in a manner that would be considered unforgivable by many.

Over the years, reports about his success were the only thing that kept her from being subdued completely by regret. Ending the engagement had pushed Gregory toward a better future, just as she had hoped. And if he resented her forever for it, she had sought comfort in the knowledge that he would be living a satisfactory life at least.

Now that he stood in front of her, the resolve she once felt drained away like a leaking bucket. She wanted to sink to her knees and beg for forgiveness. It took every bit of her willpower to keep from doing so.

"What existed between us was real," Liana said instead. "The feelings ... the passion ... all of it."

A flash of anger crossed his eyes, the first agitated emotion to appear so far on his face. "In the end, those so-called feelings weren't significant enough for you to align yourself with a member of the impoverished gentry."

"Gregory, I—"

"Let's not speak of this again," he said brusquely. "I suggest you return to the manor and get your foot inspected further, Lady Liana."

Before she could say anything else, Gregory walked away in long, fluid strides, looking every bit like the shrewd, wealthy businessman he was rumored to have become.

* * *

"I'm not surprised by any of this," Dora declared after Liana had finished recounting her latest encounter with Gregory. "He was always a proud man."

"He was?" Liana questioned, blinking in puzzlement. The constantly smiling, humble gentleman she'd fallen in love with years ago had been anything but haughty.

Dora nodded. "Most certainly, but I don't blame you for not noticing. He let his guard down whenever you were present, and his partiality to you was rather obvious. In saying this, my intention is not to be judgmental. You know how much I like to make assessments regarding other people's personalities. Truthfully, I consider being proud a necessary trait—as humans, we all require a healthy dosage of pride to live a good life."

"I feel sick and prickly all over," Liana confessed, dabbing at her sweaty forehead with a handkerchief. "Perhaps I should call for a cup of water."

The two women occupied one of the curved balconies at the back of the house, overlooking the lush gardens and a seemingly endless spread of fertile land with mountains peeking out far ahead. It was a breathtaking view, teeming with nature and air so fresh it traveled through one's lungs effortlessly. Had the situation been different, Liana would have allowed herself to enjoy the tranquil atmosphere in preparation for the intermingling soon to follow in the evening, when the last of the guests had arrived. Instead, she found herself inwardly replaying the conversation with Gregory and wincing over how awfully it had gone.

"Are you thirsty?" Dora asked in concern.

"No. However, I can't help but feel that drinking water might alleviate some of my stress."

"It won't," Dora replied, clucking sympathetically. "I'm afraid the guilt is what's making you this way. Get rid of it and you'll feel so much better."

"How do I do that?" Liana asked, touching the handkerchief to her forehead again.

"It doesn't help that you already apologized," her sister said disappointedly. "Now you've lost the advantage of being mysterious. I am familiar with men like Mr. Holt, probably because I have a similar personality myself. Loyal and doting to the ones we love, but not likely to freely extend forgiveness after being slighted."

"In spite of his evident dislike of me, he advised that I get my foot seen to upon my return."

"He's a gentleman, not a savage," Dora said bluntly, rolling her eyes. "A lack of concern towards you would be completely rude and downright scandalous. Did you do as he suggested?"

"I had Mrs. Gilbert take a look at it," Liana answered, referring to their capable housekeeper who had some medical experience. "My foot is perfectly functional, thankfully."

"Wonderful. You'll need all your limbs if you plan to successfully get through the summer," Dora responded, snuggling deeper into a beige woolen shawl wrapped over her shoulders. "Oh, I never should have given you that dastardly advice!"

After learning about Russell's letter to Gregory, Liana had gone to Theodora seeking her input. She had been certain that she would never forgive herself if Gregory abandoned his innermost desires merely to please her. If any sacrifice was to be made, she would much prefer that it come from her. "A stubborn man like that won't just leave without further prodding," Dora had announced somberly. "If you truly wish to succeed in sending him toward his promising destiny in Brazil, then you'll have to resort to saying something hurtful and drastic."

The plan had worked correctly for enabling Gregory's departure, but now it offered little aid in navigating his return.

Liana tucked a healthy strand of chestnut hair behind her ears. "You mustn't blame yourself for that. I was the one who made the decision in the end."

"I should have known you would crumble under the weight of such a heavy choice. Just one encounter and you're already so frazzled."

"I didn't expect to see him so suddenly. I was stupefied, to say the least."

"Hm," Dora said, staring at her analytically. "Do you still have feelings for him?"

The answer was so clear it felt almost pointless to say it out loud. She had never stopped loving Gregory. The pain of existing without him grew more tolerable as the months passed, but the memories from their time together still hovered persistently in her mind. On several occasions when a gentleman approached her to express romantic interest, she instinctively found herself comparing him to Gregory. Either he wasn't as sweet and romantic, or his expression didn't seem fixated enough whenever she was in his line of sight. Or he didn't utter her name in the manner Gregory used to, each syllable uttered in a tone so affectionate it sent pleasant thrills dancing along her spine.

"Will my response matter? He already thinks I'm an entitled trollop," she replied sullenly.

"Of course! We need to determine your state of mind before we arrive at the next course of action."

"I love him dearly. I always have," Liana shared in a lowered voice, shy about overtly expressing her innermost feelings.

Dora clapped her hands together triumphantly as if to signal that the matter was already resolved. "Why not tell him the truth then? If he learns that you sacrificed your own happiness to see him achieve success, he'll cease being difficult."

"He has no reason to believe me," Liana responded. "As far as he's concerned, I'm the woman who ended our engagement for conceited reasons."

A crafty smile appeared on Dora's face. "What if we showed him otherwise?"

"What do you mean?" Liana asked, blinking in confusion.

Dora reached out and patted Liana's hand encouragingly. "We'll make him see how genuine an individual you are. Believe me, if Mr. Holt insists on remaining blind to the purity of your character, he's bound to regret it for the rest of his life!"

Chapter Three

With the aid of a valet, Gregory changed out of his traveling clothes, opting for a combination of dark blue and white clothing with perfectly tailored measurements. He adjusted the collar of his shirt, engulfed by a multitude of ideas in his head. He considered his duties and pursuits, determining his next course of action.

He was an unrepentant multitasker, a proclivity many considered burdensome, whereas he wielded it as a useful skill. Most people found themselves stressed by the prospect of handling multiple tasks at the same time, but Gregory's expert grasp of organization and leadership allowed for flawless delivery across a span of lucrative projects.

He and his brother Russell had been aged thirteen and sixteen respectively when their father, Lord Campden, died from consumption and left Gregory's uncle, Albus, to serve as the guardian of his estate. Albus had proven himself to be an ineffectual caretaker whose poor financial management had run the estate into utter bankruptcy. By the time Gregory and Russell came of age, there had been nothing but dissatisfied tenants and meager crop yields to inherit.

A trust set apart for education made it possible for the Holt siblings to attend Cambridge. It was there that Gregory shed his idle innocence in preparation for a lifetime of hard work. He indulged occasionally in classical subjects like philosophy and history, but his true passion lay in trade and commerce. Gregory was certain that in the near future, there would be a widespread adoption of efficient technology that would positively transform the British economy. Like any wise businessman, he had begun positioning himself to reap significant benefits when that time came.

It was for that reason that he had chosen to travel down to Suffolk, although the demands of hosting would likely result in reduced access to Alex, Lord Radnor's attention. The earl was both a close friend and a valued business partner who also shared the belief that relying primarily on one's inherited land assets was an imprudent practice. Smart peers instead diversified their avenues of income, guaranteeing a solid pathway for expanding their estates.

Seeing Liana again had caused old memories to resurface. It brought Gregory much disappointment to discover that she was still as beautiful and soft-spoken as ever, those soulful honey eyes successfully hiding the abominable personality beneath. He had loved her once, so passionately that he would've given his life for her if she requested it. She was his first and only romantic experience, and his feelings had been so intense it defied logic.

And what had he received in return for such devotion? A biting declaration that he was not enough and would never be.

Gregory made final adjustments to his cravat and went to the door. He was determined that his interactions with Liana would be limited to necessary encounters only. That was the condition he'd agreed to with Radnor, and, moreover, conversing with Liana would only elicit more emotions from him than he cared to indulge. He had long since evolved from his past days of evocative phrases and cloying sentimentality. If anything, he let his calculating mind guide his decisions nowadays, placing self-interest above other frivolities.

Striding along the spacious hallway, Gregory realized he was looking forward to joining the other guests in the dining hall. The manor's cooks were arguably the best in the country, and their foremost delicacy, the beef consommé, was smoothly textured and abundantly flavorful. In addition, there would be dozens of wealthy gentlemen in attendance, some of whom he planned on acquainting with quality investment opportunities.

As he approached the end of the corridor, he found Alex standing by a row of expertly drawn topographical paintings.

"Well, I'm glad you don't seem put out about returning to the estate," Alex said, his words accompanied by a friendly pat on Gregory's shoulder. "It wouldn't hurt to have another marksman in the pheasant hunting group."

"Why would I be put out?" Gregory asked with a quizzical look. "Ravenmoore is, and will always be, a pleasant sight for sore eyes."

Alex paused, apparently debating whether to speak more on the subject before deciding against it. "Come," he said instead. "Let us have a quick discussion in my private study. I want to hear all about this new business idea of yours."

A few seconds later, the two men were seated on opposite sides of an expansive mahogany desk.

"Recently, Russell and I hired a geologist," Gregory began, getting right to the topic. "We wanted to determine if minerals of value existed on our family's parkland in Lancashire."

"And what did you discover?" Alex asked, his voice tinged with interest.

"The land is abundant with iron ore, spattered in clumps across two hundred acres. Many parts aren't easily extractable. That's an obstacle we intend to overcome without destructive mining."

"Congratulations, dear friend, but how do you plan to do that?" Alex questioned, ever a practical man. "If you intend to assess those minerals, you'll need to make a trade-off. Iron ore in exchange for significantly damaged land."

"Not necessarily," Gregory countered, his nerves coiling in excitement. "Whilst in London, I happened to encounter a disgruntled scientist. His latest invention, a steam-powered pump used in mining, had just been rejected by a financier on account of," he made air quotes with his fingers, "a lack of demand."

"Wouldn't be the first time such has occurred."

"Nor the last," Gregory replied agreeably. "However, upon further prodding, I realized that the prospective deal had likely fallen through due to the scientist's inability to clearly explain why his invention differed from current mining equipment."

"Ah, the old rhetorical crutch," Alex said sympathetically. "Perhaps it might have benefited him to hire an effective solicitor."

Gregory shook his head. "He could not afford it. Meanwhile, I have always been a lover of new inventions, particularly groundbreaking ones, and therefore I succeeded in convincing him to test his steam-powered pump at my parkland. Its effectiveness was obvious by a large margin," he paused to let the information sink in, then continued. "Using a boiler and a steam cylinder, this brilliant machine diverts water from deep mines, allowing for efficient and safe mining."

"That sounds like quite a revolutionary device," the earl said with admiration. "From your enthusiasm, I presume you are considering starting a manufacturing company."

"Precisely. I have already purchased exclusive rights to the steam-powered pump in a lengthy contract that cost me quite a hefty sum. However, I'm confident that the manufacturing company, once begun, will earn triple that amount in its first year."

"Wonderful. What role do I play in this?"

"I need a partner. Someone capable and fastidious, willing to invest equal amounts of financing and time. There's no other person I would consider perfect for the task."

He and Alex jointly owned another profitable establishment, a textile company specializing in durable fabric for clothing, upholstery, and household items. Not only did the two men hold a mutual respect and care for each other, but they both possessed a great deal of an element vital to thriving economic collaborations: trust.

"Manufacturing is undoubtedly an occupying field of work. I have already organized my—"

"—yearly schedule," Gregory finished with a grin. "Would it kill you to invite even the slightest bit of unpredictability into your life?"

"Probably not," Alex admitted easily as he checked his watch and rose to his feet. "But I don't desire to change. Grant me a few days to consider your proposition, will you? Now we had best head downstairs. I don't like to keep my guests waiting."

Walking closely behind Radnor, Gregory descended a spiral stairway that led to the grand hall where an elegant crowd had assembled. A few ladies tittered excitedly at the sight of the earl, who at once began pairing guests in relation to social status, shared interests, and other particularities.

Gregory's gaze swept idly across the crowd. Although he enjoyed savory dinners, he could hardly wait for the night to be over, giving way to a vibrant day laden with activity. There were a few trade contracts requiring his rapt attention, a group pheasant hunt was scheduled for the next afternoon, and he had yet to write an update letter to his brother in London. He liked keeping busy, safe in the knowledge that his efforts unfailingly resulted in tangible results.

"Mr. Holt. I didn't realize you were here," Dora Foxworth exclaimed, donning a curiously sweet smile as she approached. "The lavish dinner events, the steady hum of voices—it brings to mind the old days, doesn't it?"

Gregory had stayed previously at Ravenmoore during the start of the year, never in the summer when the hunting parties began, and therefore had no such memories as Dora suggested. "My lady," he replied truthfully. "It most certainly doesn't."

Dora seemed puzzled by his reply for a second before a look of understanding crossed her face. "You were never present at the past festivities," she murmured, tapping her forehead in a decidedly unladylike manner. "I'm not sure why I happened to forget that."

The disappointment in Dora's voice was comical, so much so that he found himself holding back a smile. He had always considered Dora like a little sister, one who possessed a sharp tongue and a kinetic personality that strongly complemented Liana's enchantingly demure self.

"We all make mistakes."

"That's right," Dora said, her confidence evidently unshaken. A challenging glint appeared in her eyes, swirling with unspoken meaning. "There are times when such blunders might seem difficult to resolve. Luckily, this summer promises to be a redeeming one. Enjoy the rest of your evening, Mr. Holt."

Only a fool would claim not to understand Dora's words, despite their probable ambiguity. Liana had clearly enlisted her sister's support in another vain effort to reclaim his favor. It was just what he expected of a coddled heiress who believed she could treat people like puppets and couldn't abide being told otherwise. Were it not for the agreement he'd made with Alex regarding keeping his distance from Liana, he would have expressed just what he thought of her obvious attempts to regain influence in his life.

He caught sight of her standing across the room, dressed in a blue silk gown that cut a shapely mold around her slender body. A line of glittering pearls circled her pale neck in an arresting sequence. Her thick curls of hair were gathered loosely in a simple chignon, and a flower-shaped pin secured it in place. She was surrounded by a group of conversing ladies, her smile warm and patient, the only one content to say little and listen with full attention.

How was it possible, Gregory wondered, that one woman could hurt him so and yet rouse such fierce attraction in his entire being? She exuded a cordial, gentle air and at the same time was capable of willful cruelty. The disparity was stark and puzzling in ways that proved difficult to understand.

Dinner was a satisfying affair featuring a mouthwatering array of meals and wine, freshly produced from the estate vineyard. Afterwards, the guests branched out into smaller groups. Some went outdoors to gather around a bonfire, a few older ladies converged in the morning room to play backgammon, and the rest proceeded to the salon to watch the hired band play.

As Gregory left the dining hall with thoughts of excusing himself for an early bedtime rest, a smiling woman stepped onto his path. Lady Emma Campbell had proven to be an intriguing seating partner; in between servings of roast venison and saffron-flavored soups, she had engaged him in a fascinating conversation on the flaws of the urban waste management system. Born to a duke who had produced only daughters, her suave confidence hinted at an auspicious upbringing where she had been encouraged to be anything but inferior.

"Do escort me to the salon, will you?" Lady Emma requested. "My mother has opted to retire early on account of a faint headache, which is rather unfortunate. I happen to enjoy things better whilst in the company of those I like."

"In that case," he replied, offering his arm, "we'll need to ensure that the night ends on a satisfactory note for you."

Lady Emma's smile broadened. "As I would expect of a refined gentleman."

He was not oblivious to the indicative lightheartedness in her tone, suggesting that she considered him more than the average conversational partner. As far as ladies went, Lady Emma sat high on the scale of desirability. Her respected familial lineage, classical blonde and blue-eyed features, in addition to an astute, sharpened mind, had led to her being zealously courted by suitors.

They were well suited, he and Lady Emma. Were they to wed each other, their union would be built on mutual respect and highbrow reasoning. No long hours spent sitting together by the lake. No melodious tunes played with a skillful hand, wedging deep within his soul. Oddly, the latter thought filled him with something close to dread.

"Do you have a flair for music?" Gregory found himself asking as they walked along the hallway.

"Unfortunately not," Lady Emma said wryly. "After years of teaching me to play the pianoforte, my music teacher was left with no choice but to grudgingly admit that I was average at best."

Gregory laughed at that. "We're similar in that regard. I, too, am inclined to appreciate exceptional music rather than attempt to produce it."

"Perfect," Lady Emma replied with a playful glance. "We already agree on the important things."

The salon was packed with ladies and gentlemen of varying ages. The atmosphere was tranquil and solemn as the band played the finishing notes of a classical sonata. Liana was seated in the back row next to the only two available chairs, and she flushed deeply as they approached.

"Lovely evening, isn't it?" Lady Emma said pleasantly to Liana as they occupied the seats.

"Indeed, it is a most delightful evening," Liana murmured. She shot an uncertain glance in Gregory's direction before turning her gaze toward the stage.

The music swelled in a rippling tide before it descended into lower notes that gradually ebbed away. Afterwards, the lead violinist, a sprightly man with a propensity for showmanship, invited members of the audience to come forward and showcase their musical talents.

Lady Emma lifted her shoulders slightly as if to say, 'Why not?' before heading toward the stage. The lead violinist had begun counting down to ten, his voice rife with unconcealed eagerness.

Turning to Liana, Gregory noticed that she didn't seem inclined to join the stage. Her expression had turned wistful, as though the ongoing display was something she lacked the permission to participate in.

Were he considered a proponent of anything, it would undoubtedly be the idea that one ought to pursue their passions as eagerly as possible. No matter the situation and shared history, pleasant or otherwise, he would always stand by that belief. And a woman like Liana, who could create mellifluous tunes on a variety of musical instruments with exact precision, fell solidly in that category.

"You should go up there," Gregory said quietly. "You're more skilled than anyone here."

Liana stiffened at the sound of his voice. A new spattering of color formed along her neck and face in a distinct flush. "I have never played in front of strangers," she replied softly.

"You let me watch you play the pianoforte merely a day after we met."

"That was different," Liana protested. "You were a rare exception."

"I believe you're afraid of negative backlash, which is an understandable concern for an artist," he continued in a practical tone. "But you'll never know the extent of your musical expertise if you don't publicly perform."

He watched as she wrestled internally with the direct sensibility of his words, floundering between the choice to heed his advice or cling to standard normalcy. Finally, she exhaled and turned to him.

"I'll do as you've suggested," she said calmly. "But only on one condition."

Gregory's gaze grew alert. "And that is?"

"I'd like a private audience with you, tomorrow morning in the private parlor. There's a lot to discuss, and if I don't seize this chance, I won't otherwise be granted the opportunity."

Gregory hesitated, considering the memories he'd formerly locked away and how burdensome it would be to open them once more. Fully aware that a positive reply could cost him a summer holiday, he nodded briefly. "Very well."

He watched as Liana walked delicately to the stage, her expression intermixed with anxiety and determination. When it was her turn to perform, her fingers strummed gracefully along the guitar strings. The music poured forth in a fast-paced, upbeat tune that would inspire even the most morose individual.

The room fell silent in hushed admiration as they listened. A smile appeared on her face, brilliant and dazzling, as she commanded undivided attention with a natural air that seemed almost foreign. It was like watching someone who had formed anew, their reticence shed amidst the flow of an encompassing performance.

The stirring display almost made the thought of the next day's arranged meeting bearable, Gregory mused. Almost.

Chapter Four

Liana had been pleasantly surprised by Gregory's encouragement to go on stage and perform for the waiting audience. He had always believed in her talents and skill more than she ever did, and even now, despite the strained tension, he had still managed to push her to put her best foot forward. Last night, she'd seen a glint of the Gregory she once knew. A man who never failed to propel others toward beneficial paths, whose propensity for altruistic acts caused him to stand out from other men. As she played, she'd felt his eyes on her. Sharp. Intense. Pushing her to give her best.

Four years ago, when she would play with him as her only audience, he would sing praises and marvel at how talented she was. Given how much he loved listening to her play, last night was the perfect prelude to the apology she planned to make today.

Sunlight streamed in through the open windows. As she prepared for the day, Liana's mind was besieged by thoughts on how her meeting with Gregory would go. She wondered if it would push him away further, if he would forgive her, if he might give her another chance.

Her dreams had been filled with memories of him. In the garden, watching her play. His fingers playing with strands of her locks. He was always tender and gentle, and, despite the passage of time, she still yearned for that softness and gentility his palms gave. It calmed her nerves more than chamomile tea ever could, and it was more soothing than a long, warm bath. She missed it. She missed him.

With the help of a maid, Liana dressed in a rose gold plain silk gown embellished with laces at the hem, perfectly complementing her skin tone. She was aware that the color was beautiful on her skin and also amplified her gentle features. Her hair was held up in a casual ponytail and secured with an almost invisible hairpin.

She hurried down the hallway to the next bedroom, belonging to her sister. Dora was lying in bed, still asleep.

"Dora, you must wake up as I am in need of advice," Liana said as she moved to sit on her sister's bed.

"What kind of advice do you need at such an ungodly hour?" Dora groaned, her eyes still shut.

"It isn't ungodly by any standard. It's dawn and the sun is already making its way up." Liana responded. She went to the window, shifting the curtains aside to let in a steady stream of light.

"Oh, for goodness' sake, shut that back." Dora groaned again, burying her head in her plush pillows.

Liana smiled and drew the curtains back together. Dora greatly valued her sleep and was more suited for evening activities than early morning discussions. However, the urgency of the situation provided a reasonable exception.

"I intend to meet with Gregory this morning at the private parlor," she divulged carefully.

Dora sprang up into a sitting position, startled by the announcement. Her onyx hair was messy and all over her face. "Truly?" she asked. "I wonder what changed his mind."

"A stroke of luck, I believe," Liana murmured, pushing a handful of Dora's hair from her face and revealing more of her beautiful features. "I am thrilled, nervous, and hopeful all at the same time."

"Things are turning out brilliantly as expected. And quickly, too. I haven't even started my scheming yet," Dora remarked with a look of satisfaction. "I know you're presently fraught with an array of emotions, but do you feel prepared to meet him at least?"

The answer to that was yes. The only thing to do, other than ignoring each other and pretending the past never existed, was to have a much-needed discussion. Although there was a risk of things growing worse as a result of unresolved grudges and heavy tension, Liana was still determined to show Gregory that she had never set out to hurt him.

"I just know we have to talk," Liana answered.

Dora's eyes softened sympathetically. She reached out to cover Liana's hands with hers. "Darling, you must know what you'll say lest you make a fool of yourself."

"What do you suggest I do, Dora?" Liana asked worriedly. "I fear he'll be significantly less inclined to listen to me. He seems rather insistent on moving on from the past."

"The fact that he agreed to meet with you proves otherwise," Dora said, her eyes bright with determination. "I think it's very simple. Tell him the truth and leave it up to him to believe you or not. If he doesn't, then that says a lot about him and the state of the union you once shared."

Liana recalled the look of disregard Gregory had given her the other day at the lake. She had hated being on the receiving end of that look and would sooner avoid experiencing that again. "I am scared about how he'll take it. I deceived him and took such an important decision without his input."

"For his own good, remember that," her sister interrupted, any remnants of sleep fully gone from her eyes. "You were trying to be supportive of him. If you had not done that, he might not be the wealthy man he is today."

"I just—I just don't want him to hate me more than he already does."

"He doesn't hate you. He's a proud man who bears some resentment, that's all. Believe me, if he hated you, he wouldn't agree to a private meeting no matter the circumstances."

With that said, Dora adjusted the collar of her blue nightdress before leaving the bed and pulling the curtains open. "What a promising day! So beautiful and devoid of mystery." She exclaimed giddily.

"You've made a rapid recovery from having your sleep interrupted," Liana noted.

"I've discovered an important piece of information, and I would appreciate it if you kept it secret as well," Dora announced with a sly grin.

"What is it?"

"There's a mysterious guest here at Ravenmoore, whose name is absent from the invitation list. Last night, I spotted him having dinner in Alexander's private drawing room."

"He might be one of Alexander's secretive billionaire friends. There are a great deal of them in England, you know."

"I fully intend to discover his identity. Perhaps it's a good thing I didn't depart for London after all."

"Have you considered asking Alexander directly?" Liana asked.

Dora shook her head. "Getting a direct answer would be no fun, and besides, our brother isn't the sort to easily divulge his secrets. I shall find the truth out myself!"

A couple of minutes later, Liana ventured into the eastern wing of the spacious manor. That part of the house had been allocated exclusively for family use, and except for the occasional passing servant, the hallways were mostly quiet and unoccupied. Her conversation with Dora had successfully granted her a dose of bravery. She felt a restless energy that demanded to be let out through conversational activity.

The door to the private parlor had been left ajar, and Liana released a quick, encouraging breath before walking in. Gregory was standing in front of the fireplace, staring at the painting of Liana's parents that hung above it. As always, he was on time and dressed impeccably in fitting clothes.

"You're late," he stated without turning around.

"I apologize," Liana murmured. "I stopped to see Dora along the way, which ended up taking more time than I anticipated."

"Then we had best not waste further time," Gregory replied, moving to occupy a plush sofa. His gaze was as sharp as a dart, never straying away from her. "Before we begin, I'd like to state that my interference last night was not borne out of a desire to reconnect. I only wished to provide needed encouragement and nothing else."

"I know that," she whispered, somehow hearing the racy thrum of her heart.

He motioned to a nearby sofa. "Now that that's been established, do share the reason why you asked for a private meeting."

For all her promises to Dora about saying the truth, Liana suddenly felt paralyzed in the face of Gregory's clear hostility. As much as she desired to let him know the true reason why their engagement had ended, she was afraid he would grow more upset at the fact that it had been a trivial case of deliberate miscommunication. One that had cost them both a world of hurt and regrets. No, Liana thought, it was much smarter to build up to it gradually.

"I want your forgiveness," she blurted out, snapping her mouth shut as soon as the words escaped.

"Do you?" Gregory asked in a cold voice, a flash of hurt and anger passing across the handsome face. "If that's what you want, then fine. I'll grant you that and nothing else."

"It's a selfish request, I know," Liana continued, her face burning with embarrassment. "We don't have to be close friends, but if we could at least get back on cordial terms—"

"You don't get it, Liana," he interrupted, the side of his mouth curving in a sardonic smile that held no hints of amusement. "I'm no longer the lovestruck boy who would come running at your behest."

She flinched, stunned by the casual bluntness of his words. In the past, he'd never spoken to her in a tone that wasn't doting or kind. It felt like a consequence of something irrevocably lost, causing a sharp pain in her heart.

Gregory rose to his feet and walked over to the door. He tried the handle a couple of times to no avail before stepping away. "It's locked," he said dispassionately. "Alexander ought to pay more attention to the state of his household furniture."

"It's an instant lock door, a gift from our uncle in France," Liana explained. "We only have to wait for a few minutes. I'm certain a maid will come by these parts soon enough."

An emotion that bordered on the edge of desperation crossed his bright green eyes. "Fine," he replied. "Let's remain here and wait."

The silence between them grew to envelop the entire room, heavy and full of unspoken conversations. "Did you ever meet that distinguished man you wanted, the one fit to marry you?"

I already have. Liana thought, feeling a strange squeeze in her chest. "After you left, I didn't get to meet anyone new, not romantically, at least."

"Why?"

She shrugged in what she hoped was a nonchalant manner. "My destiny didn't factor that in, I suppose."

Gregory's expression was doubtful. "I find it hard to believe that a beautiful woman like yourself, with a strong familial heritage, would have difficulties finding a suitor to marry her."

She averted her eyes, deciding to change the topic instead. "What about you? Why haven't you gotten married?"

He paused for a long time, seeming to think the question through before replying, "I don't know."

The sheer honesty in his tone energized her and filled her with more bravery. "Even when you were gone, I couldn't keep myself from caring for you," she divulged, her cheeks flaming as bright as a cherry. She dipped a hand into her reticule, bringing out sheets of printed paper. "I kept news clippings of you over the years, and I've been immensely proud of your success."

Gregory took the news clippings and glanced through them, a look of surprise etched across his face. When he handed the papers back to her, his body language seemed more open to conversation.

"Have you been carrying this around?"

"No," Liana replied, laughing quietly. "I just happened to bring them along with me today."

He accepted her reply with a nod, his presence exuding an air of comfort and safety merely by standing next to her.

"When I boarded the ship to Brazil, I didn't have any friends or acquaintances around for company," Gregory said, his narration tinged with nostalgia. "I was surrounded by strangers and had nothing else with me except a tiny sum of money and a great deal of trust in Russell."

"Did you know the man your brother asked you to meet?"

Gregory shook his head. "All I knew was that Russell had arranged for the importation of raw materials from Brazil to England before his arrest. If he didn't retrieve those goods, he would lose a great deal of money. I had to make the journey to avoid such a great loss."

Liana's mouth twisted in a sad smile. "It can't have been easy, leaving home for an unfamiliar place."

"It wasn't," he admitted. "Months of grueling labor and seemingly endless weeks at sea. But by the time I returned to England, Russell and I were wealthy men."

"You're young by societal standards—merely in your late twenties, and yet you have achieved more than most people can claim," she praised.

He didn't seem taken by the compliment. "Perhaps. The process of making money is a dangerous incline to venture. At some point, it no longer becomes about profit. Instead, it becomes an obsession, an endless cycle that's hard to exit from."

"But that's not the case with you," she responded. "You're far too smart an individual to be amenable to such a lifestyle."

As she spoke, she was aware of Gregory's towering physique as he drew nearer. He was an exquisite specimen of a man, and if there were any flaws in his face or body, they were either minuscule or not noticeable to the average person. His near presence turned her bones into jelly, and it took considerable effort to stand steadily.

"Is that really true?" Gregory whispered in her ear, his warm breath causing a pleasant thrill to spread across her whole body. "It's been four years, Liana. I'm no longer the man you once knew."

She was filled with a myriad of emotions, all satisfying and delicious. Yearning ... excitement ... nostalgia ... love. She had prayed for this moment since the day Gregory rode off furiously from the estate. A day when he would come to look at her with the same affection as before.

He was going to kiss her, Liana thought as he traced her cheek with his thumb and continued to close the distance between their faces. She had missed his scent. A blend of leather and wet wood, but now there was something more exquisite to it. It was unconventional yet comforting, now with an additional essence of grandeur and wealth. She could not figure out what it was, but it was not a commonplace scent. Oh, he really was going to kiss her—

The door swung open with a noticeable sound, jolting them out of the sweet moment they had been lost in. A petite maid carrying a cleaning bucket paused mid-stride, her eyes wide with surprise.

"Apologies, my lady!" She called out before hurriedly leaving the room.

Liana bit her lip to keep from crying out in protest as Gregory stepped away. He adjusted the collar of the coat and ran a hand through his hair. He looked just as affected as she was, his breathing fast and unmeasured.

"For what it's worth, I understand why you did it," Gregory said, walking over to the window and putting more distance between them. "Why you ended our engagement. You did what you had to do to further uphold your family's reputation. I cannot entirely hold that against you. In fact, I rather admire the blunt, cut-throat decision."

"Gregory," Liana said, shaking her head. "That isn't why I—"

"It's almost as impressive as your calculated effort to wedge yourself back into my life," Gregory continued, unaffected by her objections. "What a relief that we were interrupted; otherwise, I might have ended up making an even greater mistake."

He was mocking her, Liana thought. Mocking her efforts to find forgiveness, mocking her efforts to reconnect. Maybe things would never change. Maybe he would always resent her for the past, and there was no point in trying to act otherwise.

She was not a woman easily moved to anger or hurt, but Liana felt a mix of both as she left the room.

* * *

Merely seconds after Liana took her leave, Gregory sank onto the carpeted floor and sighed deeply. After being away from her for so long, all he'd wanted to do was hug her close and feel her soft, honey-like skin. A lot had changed from the past. He was finally a man worthy of a Foxworth, and if he was vain or desperate enough, he would have accepted Liana's apology without a second thought. But even amidst the haze of want and desire, he couldn't forget the forceful tragedy of her betrayal.

The realization that no matter what, he would still always want to touch her, hold her, and soothe himself with her presence nearly drove him mad. She still smelled the same, a scented mix of rose and lavender with a fruity undertone. A distinct scent, made uniquely by a talented woman who lived in the neighboring village. It was heady and intoxicating, and it punishingly stirred memories from the past when their life together had been one of bliss.

Although his request was well-meaning, Alex had invariably acted rashly by requesting that Gregory visit his estate. There was simply too much history and unsettled conflict to expect that everything would turn out uneventfully.

He had long since transformed from the sweet-faced young man who allowed himself to be vulnerable on occasion. He had risen to greater heights precisely because of his ability to conceal his thoughts, negotiate, and acquire beneficial contracts. He hadn't felt this affected and frustrated in a long while. Clearly, being around Liana shrank him into a version of his former self, and that alone was reason enough to stay away from her.

Alex had requested more time to consider the proposed business idea, but that was no longer possible. Gregory stood up and walked out of the parlor with purposeful strides. He was going to find Alex and insist on a quick answer. And once all arrangements were made, he intended to depart for London as early as possible.

Chapter Five

As leading aristocrats in the area, the Foxworths had always aided the local villagers with necessary support. This included food, gift parcels, and monetary assistance. The Foxworth siblings had endeavored to carry on the traditions, and Liana found that there was nothing more satisfying than bringing smiles to other people's faces.

She often went on these scheduled visits to the village with Dora, but this time she was going alone. Since the drastic conversation with Gregory the other day, Liana had kept to herself, skipping social events to retreat to her bedroom. She was leaving the manor now in search of solace away from all the hum and activity. It would do well to have some peace and quiet while she reflected on her discussion with Gregory.

No matter how much she tried, she couldn't shake off his last statement to her: *It's almost as impressive as your calculated effort to wedge yourself back into my life.*

Had she really been calculating and making devious plays for his heart? Liana didn't think so. If anything, she was too consumed by her feelings, which led her to be overwhelmingly impulsive. Yet, she understood why Gregory might easily mistake her passion for manipulation. Given the past, it was reasonable for him to be wary and critical.

However, her awareness of the dynamics in their relationship didn't make the truth any easier to swallow. His accusations hurt deeply, perhaps even worse than the new blunt aspect of his personality.

As she rode on a horse-drawn cart filled with piles of items for the villagers' consumption, Liana breathed the fresh air in and let her brown locks blow freely in the wind. Being outside brought much relief; her solitary time provided an escape from the whirlwind of emotions she felt. Her heart, on the other hand, ached dully from the spiteful words thrown at her.

Perhaps Gregory hated her completely, Liana thought with an internal tremor. Perhaps he hated her irrevocably, and there was no way of changing that. The thought was accompanied by a feeling of dread so great it nearly made her vomit.

The villagers were pleased by her visit, and they showed their appreciation by styling her hair into intricate braids and inviting her into their homes. Liana accepted the offer of ginger tea, and although it did not taste as rich as the ones prepared by the manor's kitchen staff, it was delightful due to the sentiment behind it.

She concluded her round of visits by calling on her friend, Evelyn. The old woman was sprightly for her age, and despite her wrinkles and speckled skin, it was easy to see that she had been a beauty in her youth. Liana admired the woman for her deep resilience, having survived the deaths of her beloved husband and their two children. Evelyn's wisdom and knack for cutting through nonsense were qualities that had drawn many to her door over the years.

Evelyn greeted Liana with a warm hug and led her inside the cozy cottage, which smelled of lavender and freshly baked cookies. Antique ornaments lined the walls, each with a story Evelyn was always happy to share.

"How's your leg now?" Liana asked as Evelyn set a plate of cookies on the table.

"Better. It's a privilege to grow old, you know. It comes with its fair share of leg aches and sore backs, but I wouldn't trade it for anything," Evelyn said, settling into her chair with a contented sigh. "Now, what brings you here, dear? You look like you've got the weight of the world on your shoulders."

Liana hesitated, her hands fidgeting in her lap. "It's … Gregory. I've been keeping something from him. Something important. But telling him might ruin everything."

Evelyn tilted her head, her sharp eyes studying Liana's face. "Ah, secrets. They're like splinters, you know. The longer you leave them, the deeper they burrow and the harder they are to remove."

Liana bit her lip, unsure how to respond.

Evelyn leaned forward, her voice soft but firm. "Liana, life is too short to carry the weight of what-ifs. You can't control how someone else reacts to the truth, but you can control whether or not you offer it. Gregory deserves to know, doesn't he?"

Liana nodded slowly. "He does. But what if he doesn't forgive me?"

"And what if he does?" Evelyn countered with a small smile. "Love isn't about perfection, my dear. It's about honesty and vulnerability. If he truly cares for you, he'll find a way to understand."

Liana's heart ached at the simplicity and wisdom of Evelyn's words. "You make it sound so easy."

"Oh, it's never easy," Evelyn said with a chuckle. "But the hardest choices are often the ones that matter most. Speak your truth, Liana. Let the chips fall where they may. You might be surprised at how strong Gregory really is."

As Liana rode back to Ravenmoore Estate, Evelyn's words echoed in her mind. The road ahead was still uncertain, but for the first time, she felt a flicker of courage. Whatever the outcome, she would face it with an open heart and the truth on her lips.

* * *

The earl had promised a stay laden with good food and interesting activities. He'd delivered on both counts, his organization of the guests so fluid and encompassing that it was hard for anyone to feel left out. The other day, the men had gone on long fishing trips where they chatted and cracked jokes over catches of trout. And this morning, Gregory had ridden a feisty thoroughbred, said to be one of Alex's best horses, as the group of men and a few women went horse riding.

Upon his return, he had joined the others in the dining hall for lunch, and now he found himself amidst the beautiful estate garden, in the company of Lady Emma.

Lady Emma took deliberate, measured steps along the gravel pathway, her parasol tilted elegantly over her shoulder. The lace trim of her lavender gown caught the sunlight, enhancing her ethereal beauty. Gregory walked alongside her with his hands clasped behind his back and the ends of his tailcoat flapping in the wind.

Although they were the only ones in the garden, they were in full view of the people who had opted to have their lunch out on the terrace. That made the obvious fact of their spending time together less scandalous, although Gregory suspected Lady Emma didn't care one way or the other if they had a chaperone. It was unfortunate, Gregory thought, that she had been born into a society where women decidedly had fewer privileges. Were she a man, he did not doubt that Lady Emma would be an active policymaker arguing for beneficial bills in the parliament or a businessman like himself, further contributing to the growth of society.

He ought to be enjoying Lady Emma's company as she passionately discussed the demerits of the recent reform bill. Instead, his thoughts drifted to a certain pair of honey-brown eyes he'd been trying and failing woefully to forget.

"You're unusually quiet today, Mr. Holt," Lady Emma commented with an observant glance at him.

"Am I?" Gregory asked with a polite smile. "Maybe I've been distracted by the beauty of the surroundings." He gestured to the rows of flowers, unabashedly casting their fragrance across the space. "They're rather nice to behold, the white roses especially."

"An excellent deflection," Lady Emma praised with a knowing smile. "But I suspect there's more on your mind than the splendor of our surroundings."

He had always prided himself on his ability to divide his attention and multitask, and he wasn't about to fail now. "You may be right, but henceforth I assure you that you have my attention."

"I wonder," she continued, tilting her head curiously. "Are you as guarded with everyone as you are with me?"

The question was unexpected and caught him by surprise. "Guarded? I prefer to think of myself as ... selective in my expressions."

"Another diplomatic response," Lady Emma teased. "However, I'll accept it. For now."

They rounded a corner, coming to a shaded grove where a small fountain trickled softly. Lady Emma gestured toward a bench beneath an ancient oak tree. "Shall we sit for a moment? I find the sound of water quite soothing."

Gregory obliged, sitting next to her with a respectful distance between them. Lady Emma twirled her parasol idly, her blue eyes watching him.

"You're an enigma, Mr. Holt," she declared after a pause.

"Am I?" He asked, amused. No one had described him in that manner before, at least not to his knowledge.

"Yes. You're driven, ambitious, and remarkably accomplished, yet there's a weight about you. A shadow that lingers."

Gregory's eyebrows shot up. "I didn't realize I was so transparent."

Lady Emma laughed. "Oh, it isn't transparent. I've spent a great deal of my life navigating the social maze of London elites. One learns to read between the lines."

"And what have you read in me?"

"I see a man who has fought hard to build himself up from ruin, but who hasn't fully let go of what brought him there. A man who carries scars beneath the surface."

Gregory's gaze hardened in automatic defense before softening, "You're quite astute, Lady Emma."

She smiled again, though this time there was a hint of sadness. "It's not difficult to see when one knows where to look."

They sat in silence for a while, the fountain's soft murmur filling the air between them. Gregory found himself appreciating Lady Emma's insight, though it made him uncomfortable. She saw too much and came too close to truths he wasn't ready to confront.

He liked her as an individual, a friend. The stoic businessman within him argued that mutual respect was the only thing he required for a successful marriage. Lady Emma respected him, and he similarly respected her. Her interest in him was rather obvious, and if they continued in that manner, their lives together would turn out quite brilliantly. But the empathetic part of him refused to doom Lady

Emma to a potentially loveless marriage when she could meet someone who appreciated every inch of her unique traits. Like he once did with Liana.

"You're thinking of someone," she said finally, breaking the quiet.

Gregory turned to her sharply. "Why do you say that?"

"I'm an excellent judge of character and disposition," Lady Emma replied, flashing him a smile. "In addition, I've noticed that when you aren't fully present, your gaze grows distant. It's almost as if your mind is elsewhere with someone who occupies more of your heart than you're willing to admit."

Her words struck him like a reverberating chord. He wanted to deny it, to argue that she was wrong and he had moved past whatever feelings lingered for Liana. But the truth, albeit inconvenient and maddening, was that Lady Emma was right.

"I don't dwell on the past," he replied gruffly, his body firm but not unkind.

"No," she replied kindly. "But it seems the past dwells on you."

Gregory grew more uncomfortable as his inner life was being accessed. He was no denier of the truth, but there was no point in exploring topics that were better left alone.

Before he could respond, Lady Emma shot him a look of apology. "I'm sorry, I must be making you uncomfortable. I assure you, that wasn't my intention at all. Perhaps my active curiosity isn't such an admirable trait."

"You aren't entirely wrong," Gregory reassured her. "Besides, I appreciate your earnestness about life, even if it involves sore subjects."

How odd, Gregory mused privately, that he was still thinking of Liana at a time like this. It was pure torture, having one's mind stuck on the same person. He couldn't keep from wondering what she was doing at the moment and what their next interaction would be like.

No doubt, Liana would withdraw from him now that he had fully expressed his thoughts about her. That was what he wanted, wasn't it?

He ran a weary hand through his hair, stifling a sigh. It was, indeed. He was counting down the hours until he could finally depart from Ravenmoore Estate. The previous day's mission to find Alex and demand an answer to his business proposal had proven futile. Alex had been too occupied with hosting duties to grant him an audience, further delaying his stay.

And in addition to that, there was also Lady Emma to consider. The young lady bore a remarkable astuteness that was rare. She was no fool—she could see that his reaction to her was more friendly than romantic. However, it seemed that detail was not enough to dissuade her.

Perhaps she was the way out of the mental puzzle he'd found himself in. Courting Lady Emma was certainly one way to move on with his life and keep from dwelling on the past. That was definitely an option worth considering.

The peaceful silence between him and Lady Emma continued, and just as he was beginning to consider breaking it, he saw Dora hurrying toward them. Gone was the playful, almost mischievous smile that often occupied her face. She looked disturbed, and her skin had turned a frightening shade of pale.

"Good heavens, thank goodness I found you," Dora rushed out.

"What's the matter?" Gregory asked, rising abruptly to his feet. He was certain now that something was out of place.

"I cannot find Liana. Have you seen her?"

"No, I haven't," he responded, making an effort to keep the worry from his voice. "Did she leave the manor?"

"She was last seen heading to the village this morning. It has been several hours since then. Liana is not the sort to delay in her errands and …," Dora paused to glance briefly at the sky, her frown deepening. "It looks like rain. There's no telling how long the rain will go on for once it begins, which is why we need to find her quickly."

His worry growing by the second, Gregory turned to Lady Emma. "I'm afraid I must ask your permission to cut our conversation short. An urgent matter requires my attention."

"Most certainly," Lady Emma replied with a look of understanding. "A missing lady is a necessary issue to be addressed."

Gregory made toward the stables to retrieve a horse for the ride into the village. Dora followed closely after him, her words reaching him through a fog of concern and rising alarm.

"I'll go with you," she said determinedly. "Two pairs of eyes are better than one. If we don't return in time, Alex will send some men after us."

"Does he know Liana is missing yet?"

Dora shook her head. "I wanted to be certain that you hadn't seen her before raising the alarm. I have spent the past hour searching the manor grounds to no avail. The only explanation is that she's stuck in the village or on the trail leading back home."

"You should head indoors and inform Alex about Liana's long absence," he said in a firm voice. "I'm going in search of Liana at once. Every second matters in situations like this one, and we need all the help we can get."

Dora nodded, not seeing a reason to dispute his line of logic. "Thank you for agreeing to help."

He was no savior, Gregory thought as he rode his horse through the woods. His actions now were purely selfish, a final attempt to patch his own bleeding heart. Without Liana to occupy it, there was no telling what he would become. *Please be safe.* He pleaded, feeling the highest levels of anxiety and fear swirling together within him.

Chapter Six

The sky began to darken as Liana journeyed further from the village. It looked like it was going to rain, the clouds gathering in darkening groups. Liana held a growing hope that she would make it home in time, until the first drop of rain splattered on her cheeks. It drew her back to reality and made her realize that might not be the case.

She began to hurry back, nudging her horse forward as much as she could, but the rain intensified gradually and transformed into a storm. The wind howled, dragging across the air and tossing branches into her path. Everything about it scared her—the whipping air, the crack of thunder, and the disorienting feel of the environment.

Spotting a rocky cave a short distance away, Liana hurried towards it for protection against the harsh weather. The cave was damp and cold, but at least it kept her from being soaked by the incoming deluge. Her gown had wrapped itself uncomfortably around her; as she untangled it, fearful thoughts flitted around in her mind. What if she got stuck here, forever? And what if the rain didn't stop falling?

She was not the sort to give in to an unreasonable, exaggerated line of thinking, but her fear was so great it ruled everything else. Since she was a child, Liana had always been afraid of storms. And now, as an adult, it took everything within her to keep from crumbling.

With another thunderous sound, the storm worsened, and the sound of intermixed rain and wind sent shock waves down her spine. It took her back to the time when her six-year-old self had joined her father on a horse ride through the woods. As they rode back home amidst a sudden storm, Liana's horse got spooked by a tree getting struck by lightning. It had reared suddenly, causing Liana to fall into the mud and injure her arm. Although her father had rushed to her rescue and tended to her wounds, the lasting damage had already established itself.

Now, every time there was a storm, Liana could hear the horse in her childhood neighing and recalled the loud noises and the fear that came with it.

To take her mind off unpleasant thoughts, Liana blinked until her eyes adjusted to the dim light. Someone had previously occupied the cave, judging by a few leftover wooden sticks and tree branches meant for starting a fire. After picking up two stones from the untidy floor, she gathered the kindling into a mound. She had never lit a fire herself. That task was typically handled by the maids and other staff in her household. But she was certain that if she struck two stones together hard enough, that was bound to yield desired results. Her fingers trembled. She managed to keep her resolve steady, but even as tiny sparks flew from the two stones striking each other, nothing close to a fire occurred. She dropped the stones and wrapped her arms around herself, her heart thudding rapidly.

The wind pushed against the cave opening with a clattering sound, carrying a familiar voice that brought her relief the moment she heard it. Maybe she was hallucinating, Liana mused with a brief shiver, thinking the cold must be messing with her mind.

"Liana!" it came again.

This time, her eyes flew open. It was faint but undeniably there. Gregory had come for her. Excited, she found the strength to jolt up to her feet and stumble towards the opening, shielding her face from the harsh force of the wind. She stepped into the rain once again, this time without a care for the wetness and cold it brought. The cold seeped into her dress, drenching her as she shielded her face from the storm and tried to pinpoint where Gregory's voice was coming from.

"Gregory!" She called out, hoping he could hear her.

Almost like a miracle, Gregory's horse burst through the woods. The animal galloped towards her, its rider upright and skillful in his steering. The sight of him inspired a flood of relief and yearning within her. Her knees buckled in weakness, and in a flurry of movement, he caught her just before she collapsed. He carried her into the cave, gripping her tightly as though she was going to disappear.

Her body felt at rest against the surprising warmth of his body. As he bent over her, their faces a few inches apart, she could see the vulnerable emotions clearly spread across his face.

"Liana." There was a clear relief in his voice, so unlike anything she had ever heard. He brought her closer, pulling her in what seemed to be a brief embrace. "I'm glad you're safe."

"I— I was hoping someone would find me. And you did," Liana muttered through chattering teeth.

"You should conserve your energy while you recover," Gregory urged, setting her down and walking over to the abandoned mound of sticks and tree branches.

She watched as he struck the stones together with a practiced hand, resulting in a burst of flame. Next, he fed the fire with more sticks to make it bigger. The situation made her recall how he could do almost anything. It had been a source of wonder for her in the past, how he knew to do things perfectly. "How did you know where I was?"

"I didn't," he said. He returned and held her in his arms, providing warmth and security in one smooth movement. "The cave was merely a place to check. If you weren't here, I would simply keep on searching."

The honesty and care in his words were surprising. The man who had seemed determined to spurn her affections was holding her so carefully as though she were fragile. He had ridden through the storm, determined to find her.

It felt like a dream. Perhaps she had truly fallen and hit her head hard. Liana closed her eyes, trying to savor every second of the sweet moment before it ended.

"What were you thinking, wandering off in this weather?" He murmured against her hair, breaking the silence. "You could have been seriously hurt or worse..." He let his voice trail off without completing the sentence. Instead, he pulled her even closer, almost as though he was scared by the unspoken thought.

"It was a clear day when I left the estate," she explained. "I've made this trip several times, and I thought today would be uneventful as usual. I was wrong. Next time, I'll take Dora along so we can face any obstacles together."

Gregory nodded in approval, gently tracing an invisible line along her wrist. "She's the best sister anyone could ever hope for. Once she noticed you were gone, she was prepared to rally the troops to find you."

Liana couldn't hold back a doting smile. "That sounds exactly like Dora."

"When I got the news that you were missing, the only conviction I had was that I needed to find you."

"Did Dora ask you to do that?"

"Yes," he replied. He paused to reposition her into a more comfortable position before continuing quietly, "But I would have gone searching for you regardless."

The air suddenly felt charged with a myriad of unspoken emotions. The tension heightened as Gregory gently turned her around so she was facing him. His eyes were darker in the dimming light, but that only added to the extraordinary quality of his gaze.

"Gregory, I ..." she began, not sure of what precisely she had meant to say. The feelings within her were too strong, too passionate to be accurately put into words. She had waited so long for this moment. A moment when Gregory would no longer glance at her with resentment or ill feelings.

"Liana." There was an urgency in his voice, a familiar one she'd not witnessed since the days of their engagement.

"Yes?"

"If you ever have to leave the manor and there's no one available to escort you, promise that you'll call on me."

The statement was delivered with some authority and a greater amount of care. "I— I will," Liana replied, still startled by the new development. If she had known being in harm's way was the catalyst toward regaining some of Gregory's affection, perhaps she might have ventured into the village a long time ago. The thought of that amused her greatly, bringing a slight smile to her lips.

Gregory nudged her with his arm. "Why are you smiling?"

"I like this," Liana admitted carefully. "I like us together like this. It brings me so much joy."

Gregory averted his eyes, staring in the direction of the fire. "A day ago, I would have hesitated to say the same. However, when I learned you were missing, all I wanted was to find you and be able to have such nice moments again."

"Your arrival saved me in more ways than one."

Gregory said nothing, raising his eyebrows slightly as an indication for her to continue.

"The realization that I was alone and stuck in the middle of a storm brought harsh memories from the past," she said. "If you hadn't arrived when you did ... there's no telling what could have happened to my state of mind."

The relief of being found by him swept over her again, warming her more quickly than the fire.

"Never again," Gregory murmured, his voice low and steady. "You will not find yourself alone in a scary situation like this one if I have anything to do with it."

She stared back at him curiously. "How will you make that happen?"

"Do not underestimate my problem-solving abilities," he answered with a voice full of challenge. "I might even install a permanent guard at your side if I have to."

Liana's lips curved in a happy smile. Earlier that day, the mere idea of her and Gregory being on good terms had seemed impossible. Now here he was, showing some of that doting trait she had once known him for. It was nothing short of a miracle.

The storm still raged outside, but here in this abandoned, tattered cave, with Gregory's calm and soothing presence surrounding her and his pleasant scent overpowering her reasoning, her world was at peace. The fire cast a warm glow across the cave, ushering in an atmosphere of blissful calm.

"Why do you care?" Liana whispered, needing reassurance that everything would be fine henceforth.

Gregory turned to her, his eyes the softest she had seen since his arrival. "Because I can't seem to stop."

They sat in silence for a few more minutes before Liana spoke again. "I need to tell you something important." Her hands fidgeted in her lap, and her formerly calm nerves betrayed her by rattling once again.

Gregory acknowledged her serious expression with a look of surprise. "Go on."

She took a deep breath, knowing what she was about to say would either improve or ruin their relationship further. "Four years ago, when I ended our engagement... I didn't do it because I thought you were unworthy. I lied about that. The truth is, I thought it was the only way to protect you."

She was aware of Gregory's intense gaze on her. The look on his face was an undeniable mix of confusion. "Protect me? From what?"

"Everything. The scandal, especially. Your family's reputation had taken a massive hit at the time," she responded, words rushing out of her lips in a tumble as though she could no longer hold it in. "Your brother's trial was a cause for whispers at gatherings and high society events. I knew leaving the country was a golden chance to improve your life. If you had stayed for my sake, it would be increasingly difficult to survive all that scrutiny."

"So, you let me go?"

"I— I thought if I let you go, you'd have a better chance in Brazil to rebuild your life without their judgments dragging you down."

He was staring at her with an indecipherable look on his face, his mouth slightly open. For a minute, Liana feared that she had made a mistake by sharing the truth at that moment. It terrified her, the thought that her confession could be the final piece destroying what was left of their relationship.

Gregory exhaled deeply, his shoulders relaxing as he leaned his back against a wall. "You choose to sacrifice us," he said quietly, his voice heavy with disbelief and obvious shock.

Liana nodded, her eyes watering. "I thought I was protecting you. I thought I was doing the right thing, but I have felt endless turmoil over my actions since you left the estate that day."

Shaking his head in disbelief, Gregory drew closer and pulled her in for a hug. "You're full of surprises. To think you could make such a decision without telling me all this while ..."

"I was foolish and young. I truly believed I was helping you and didn't know how else I could have."

She listened to the steady hum of Gregory's heartbeat as his hand caressed her hair. When he spoke again, his voice was soft and full of emotion. "You were wrong, Liana. I was always full of ambition, and I would have gained success one way or the other. However, I cannot help but admire your intentions. It was truly selfless."

"You mean that?" she asked, relieved that he wasn't upset.

"I do. I apologize for the awful things I have said to you in recent days. You do not deserve my anger."

Liana smiled kindly. "You have more than made up for that by coming here."

Gregory smirked. "I guess old habits die hard."

"I have missed this doting personality of yours, now hidden under the canopy of your ambitions."

"It still exists in many ways," he reassured her. "I'm still the same man who is competitive at games and hunting. I still enjoy speaking to you and seeing a smile on your face."

"Well, that's a relief."

Her sheer honesty elicited a round of amused laughter from Gregory. She inhaled deeply, letting his heady scent occupy her lungs. They had many years of conversations to catch up on, and the idea of doing that was incredibly welcome. She had several unanswered questions relating to his life—how he had begun his businesses, and how he had established himself upon his return from Brazil.

As if he had been reading her mind, Gregory began speaking about the past. He told her a funny story about how he had convinced investors to fund his business idea with one well-placed joke. He also shared anecdotes about the time he spent at sea.

"And your brother? I hope he's well," Liana said. Although she had yet to meet the man, he was known to be a controversial figure who often garnered mixed reactions.

"Russell's quite well," Gregory answered pleasantly. "He's established quite an enviable life for himself."

"But?" she pressed, sensing that there was more.

"I believe my brother's scandal, although now resolved, may have been initiated by my uncle."

"The one who mismanaged your father's estate?"

He nodded with a grim expression. "The very same. He seems to be interested in eliminating my brother and me, leaving room for him to inherit the estate."

Gregory was a thoughtful man, and he was not inclined to make unwarranted accusations. Although she had not been told the details, Liana believed him.

"Part of the reason I'm here at Ravenmoore is to launch yet another business, one that's separate from the properties we inherited. Given my suspicions, I thought it would be best to establish our fortunes independently."

"He sounds like quite an awful man," Liana said. "Is there a reason why you haven't confronted him yet?"

Gregory's frown deepened. "Presently, I do not have sufficient proof to prosecute him. All I possess is a hunch. However, my private investigator is working on it. I intend to confront him when I have the evidence."

"I hope you succeed in bringing your uncle to book for his schemes."

They fell again into a comfortable silence, just as the rain slowed to a gentle patter. The atmosphere was layered in a natural quiet, and the sounds of chirping birds could be heard in the distance.

Gregory rose to his feet and extended a hand out to her. "Come, let's go to the manor before a search party is launched on our behalf. Do you have the strength to ride your horse, or will you ride with me?"

"I think I should ride with you." She took his hand, glad to feel the warmth of his touch on her skin. Together they stepped into the damp, cool air, the bond between them stronger than it had been days ago.

As violent as the storm was, it had succeeded in mending a bond that had been broken for over four years. Liana released a satisfied sigh, leaning against Gregory's firm chest as they rode back to the manor on his horse, her own horse following. Eleanor had been right after all. Just as the old lady had predicted, she had freed herself from internal turmoil and garnered good tidings by revealing the truth.

* * *

Upon their arrival at the manor, Liana was promptly swept away by a relieved Dora and chiding Radnor. In the privacy of his room, Gregory read a newly delivered letter from Russell. His brother had written that their uncle Silas was aware of their plan to separate their fortunes from the familial inheritance and had begun working to sabotage them.

His brows creased at the information, and his expression darkened. He felt a new wave of annoyance spread across his body, subduing it with measured breaths. Gently, he folded the letter and placed it on the wooden desk nearby.

His uncle was free to scheme as he wanted. It was only a matter of time before his deceitful tricks would be brought to light. Meanwhile, he had best hurry his plans along. There was still a great deal of planning to execute before the manufacturing company could be brought to life.

Gregory walked to the window, taking in the pleasurable sights that made Ravenmoore Estate a popular destination. When he had first arrived, all he had wanted was to be away from Liana Foxworth. After today, he was certain it would take a lot to keep thoughts of her from endlessly occupying his mind.

Her confession in the cave had transformed everything, and he was unsure of how to proceed. One thing was certain: she had meant what she said during their earlier meeting and never stopped caring.

He and Liana were lucky to have found each other so early in life, and now they were lucky to have reconnected again. The future suddenly seemed more expansive, spreading into new avenues for joy and fulfillment.

Chapter Seven

The warmth of the tea seeped through the porcelain cup. It radiated from Liana's hands through her entire body, comforting her and easing any leftover stress from the events of the previous day. She was still a bit chilled, but Dora had created a massive mountain of pillows and blankets that kept her warm all night and made her feel much better.

She had dreamt about Gregory all night. His warmth encircling her, his scent intoxicating her, and his arms enclosing her in a memorable embrace. In the dream, he professed his love to her over and over again, telling her how much he missed her and how much he disliked the idea of being away from each other. Then the rays from the morning sun filtered through her window and his voice drifted away. She had woken up to find herself tucked in her bed, surrounded by warmth and the realization that the dream had come to an end.

Dora had visited at the break of dawn to confirm that Liana had slept well and had urged her to rest some more, then departed to have breakfast. The maids delivered Liana's breakfast directly to her room. She propped herself against the mountain of pillows on her bed, her hair cascading over her shoulders in an unhindered tumble. After being drenched the previous day, Liana found that she had gained a new appreciation for warmth and dryness.

She was tucked comfortably between soft blankets that offered solace from the chill that had formerly settled deep in her bones. She took a sip of her tea, savoring the sweet blend of honey and chamomile, and was grateful for the glorious moment of reprieve.

When Dora returned, she looked pleased to find Liana sitting up in bed. As if sensing that Liana needed some time to appreciate the calm morning, Dora settled on a sofa next to the window and snuck occasional glances at the landscape before sketching determinedly on a notepaper. The steady scratching of her pen filled the silence, mixing with the cracking of the fireplace and the sound of Liana sipping her tea.

Once it was clear that the silence was beginning to transition into boredom, Dora set her notepaper aside and turned to Liana with a smile.

"You look better," Dora declared. "Much better than what I have been drawing, at least."

Liana smiled. "Did you just compare me to a piece of hastily drawn artwork?"

"It appears so," her sister replied with a matching smile. "There are worse things to be compared to, believe me."

"In any case, I'm all better thanks to you. You have always been an exceptional and persistent nurse, but you've outdone yourself this time."

"How so?"

"By insisting I remain wrapped up in this mountain," Liana said, motioning to the blankets. "And the hot tea. At this pace, I shall feel human again before dusk."

"Well, I couldn't have my dear little sister falling apart," Dora replied with a satisfied air. "Especially not when Gregory Holt's been hovering about like a brooding knight, ready to swoop in at the first sign of trouble."

"What ... what do you mean?" Liana asked, unable to hide her excitement. A part of her had been afraid that Gregory would revert to his antagonistic self, so the knowledge that he was still as doting as he'd been yesterday pleased her greatly.

"It's true, is it not? He swooped in to save you from the storm and brought you back like a knight in shining armor," Dora said with a teasing glint in her eyes. "Only today, I have had to contend severely with his inquiries about the state of your health."

A bright blush began spreading across Liana's face. "Truly?"

"Most certainly. You know I wouldn't joke about that without reason. The man wandered through a raging storm in order to find you. If that doesn't scream undying devotion, I don't know what does."

"It isn't like that," Liana protested shyly, her face growing redder. She didn't want to give the impression that they had reignited their earlier relationship, although the idea of that seemed heavenly. "He was ... concerned for me. That was all."

"Hm," was all Dora said, her doubt clearly expressed through her facial expression. "Well, he was certainly concerned enough to have left Lady Emma in the garden all by herself. He wasted no time in running to find you."

Liana's eyes widened. "What? Truly?"

Dora nodded proudly. "That's right. Speaking of Lady Emma, I was not aware she and Mr. Holt were such good friends."

"I spotted them together on a previous occasion," Liana responded. "She seems enraptured by him, but I'm not entirely sure what his affections for her are."

"One thing's for certain: if she likes him, then he isn't entirely clueless about her feelings. Lady Emma isn't the sort to mince her words and play the role of the shy, reserved lady."

"I admire that aspect of her personality," Liana said quietly. "A part of me can see how well-suited she is to Gregory."

"Hush," Dora admonished, leaning closer. "It appears you are clueless about how much he still cares for you. He left her without a second thought, just to find you."

"But—"

"No buts! I will not let you create room for doubt. Permit me to tell you this in detail. When he learned the news of your disappearance, he jumped to his feet, offered a brief apology, and without waiting for Lady Emma's response, he ran to fetch a horse and hurried to find you," Dora narrated with a dreamy sigh. "It was wonderful to watch. It seemed he couldn't bear another second of not knowing where you were."

Liana couldn't help a smile from spreading across her face as she listened to her sister's words. "I still think it was out of concern. After our former encounter, he likely felt responsible for my wandering off."

That drew Dora's attention. "You never did tell me what happened at the private parlor. Did you tell him the truth? What did he say to that?"

"No, I unfortunately didn't," she replied, glancing down at her hands. "He was resentful about the past, and it felt ill-timed to share such a big secret."

"That's understandable," Dora said supportively, although it was clear that she was disappointed by the answer. "In any case, it is clear that Mr. Holt is more interested in you than he cares to admit. His decision to go rescuing you proves that."

"I'm not finished, Dora," Liana said gently, eager to share more of the recent developments.

"Oh, there's more?"

"When we were sheltering in the cave during the storm, I gathered enough courage to tell the truth about why I had ended our engagement."

Dora's eyes widened in surprise, and she eagerly moved from her seat in the corner to the foot of Liana's bed. "And how did that go?" She asked eagerly. "What did he say?"

"To my surprise, he took it quite well," Liana shared, taking another sip of her tea in a bid to finish it before it got cold. "He chastised me gently for keeping such a decision secret, but he also called it selfless. As I recall, there was a mix of surprise and amusement on his face."

"Amusement?" Dora asked, confused.

"Well, I guess I wouldn't exactly call it amusement ... but it was certainly the opposite of being angry."

"What exactly did he say?"

"He expressed that he admired my intentions even though he disagreed with the decision. I don't think I'll ever again make such a decision without speaking to him about it. He also apologized for the unkind statements he'd made," Liana said, smiling as she recalled the sweet memories from the previous day. "I believe we're beginning to understand each other again."

"This is wonderful news," Dora said, rearranging her position to sit upright. A satisfied smile had begun playing on her face. "About time that happened. I knew he would come around eventually. All you needed to do was be honest with him."

"Thank you for the well-meaning advice, Dora ..."

The flow of conversation was interrupted by a firm knock on the door. Upon Dora's answering call, the door opened slightly to reveal Alex, his tall frame backlit by the warm glow of the hallway.

"I'm accompanied by guests. Are you properly dressed?"

"I am," Liana responded. Just before she had begun drinking her tea, her personal maid had helped her into a modest satin gown.

"You look lovely as always, dear sister," Alex said amiably, nudging the door wider. "Given the tiring state of the previous day's affairs, I thought it would be best to pay you a visit instead of expecting you to leave the room. Holt and Mr. Barrow here agreed with the idea."

Liana's heart gave a little leap as her eyes fell on Gregory. He looked extra handsome in a dark tailcoat and his hair tidily combed. His expression softened significantly as he gazed at her with eyes filled with care. The other man was Edwin Barrow, an influential middle-aged man who had never declined the yearly summer invitations to Ravenmoore Estate. Her interactions with him were strictly casual, which led her to wonder why he had come to pay her a visit.

"How are you feeling?" Gregory asked softly.

"Significantly better, all thanks to you," she replied, recalling how it had felt to be enclosed within those strong arms hidden beneath his neatly tailored clothes.

"And my insistence on the blankets," Dora added humorously. "As well as the band of men Alex organized to find you ... although due to Gregory, that wasn't of much use."

"Yes, my profound thanks to everyone. Gregory especially," Liana amended with a witty smile.

"That's good to hear," Alex replied. "I thought it best to bring Holt along to ensure he sees that I wasn't exaggerating your recovery."

"A fundamental rule for any businessman is to always validate statements," Gregory responded, his gaze lingering on Liana. "I'm more than relieved to have seen the truth for myself."

Clearing his throat to draw attention, Mr. Barrow stepped forward with a confident stride and a knowing smile. He was a man of connections, particularly in the arts, and his arrival at Ravenmoore was always accompanied by murmurs about opportunities and golden chances.

"Lady Liana, it's nice to see you looking so well," Mr. Barrow greeted warmly. "I don't mean to intrude. I heard about your harrowing adventure in the storm and thought it best to check on you. In addition, I have news that may be of interest."

The room fell quiet as everyone glanced at the older man expectantly. Mr. Barrow had provided Dora with several opportunities to show her artwork in renowned galleries and shows. Liana wondered what news he could have that would be of interest to her.

Liana tilted her head curiously. "News?"

"Yes," Mr. Barrow said, clearing his throat. "As you know, my work frequently takes me across the Atlantic. I have recently returned from America, where I had the pleasure of meeting several prominent figures in the musical world."

Mr. Barrow stepped further into the room, his eyes twinkling with enthusiasm. "Lady Liana, I must confess that your reputation precedes you. I heard whispers of your remarkable skill with the pianoforte on the evening of my arrival. It seems your talent has an undeniable way of leaving an impression on others."

Dora's eyes glinted in obvious excitement. Liana blinked in surprise, her eyes darting between a pleased-looking Alexander and a waiting Mr. Barrow. She was unsure that she had heard him correctly.

"You flatter me, Mr. Barrow. I hardly think my modest performance warrants such praise."

"Nonsense!" he exclaimed, his tone rich with conviction. "Few people have the power to captivate in the way that you do. It would be a crime to refrain from showering you with deserved praise. Your skill is unforgettable. While I was in New York, a colleague informed me that he was in search of fresh talent for his theater company. I believe you're exactly the sort of person he's been seeking."

"Truly?"

Mr. Barrow nodded vigorously. "Indeed. He needs someone with an exemplary talent for instruments. Someone who enchants the audience with a moving performance. On his behalf, I hereby invite you to join his theater and embark on a fulfilling career in America." He concluded as though it was a normal thing to invite unmarried women to start a career in America, as if they could just leave the next day without a care in the world.

Liana processed his words, still unable to completely make sense of them.

"And what sort of theater company does this colleague of yours run, Mr. Barrow?" Dora asked, drawing her chair closer with interest.

"Excellent question, Lady Dora," Mr. Barrow replied, tipping his head in acknowledgement as he turned to face her. "It is one of the most innovative theatres I have encountered in New York. They combine classical and contemporary performances, blending music, drama, and dance to captivate the audience. It is a bold endeavor and, might I say, enchanting."

The room fell quiet as the earnestness of his word settled over them. Liana glanced at Dora, whose expression was a mix of surprise and excitement, before managing a glance at Gregory. His face betrayed nothing, but the slight tension in his jaw did not escape her notice.

Liana hesitated, her hands clasped under her blanket. "A career in theatre," she repeated slowly, as if testing the idea on her tongue. "In America."

"Yes," Mr. Barrow said. "It would be a bold step, one with a rather high chance of leading to great success. You have the talent, my lady. This is an opportunity to showcase that on an international stage."

"That sounds fascinating, but surely there are more performers more qualified than I."

"I've been told that they have an inclination toward natural talent, and as you may guess, their performances aren't typical. Talent like yours is rare to come by," Mr. Barrow affirmed.

Liana's heart raced as the possibilities unfolded in her mind. A career in music and theater had seemed impossible, more so because she had refrained from performing publicly. Yet here it was, days after her first public performance, and presented to her in the most expected way.

"You mentioned that this opportunity would be in America," Alex said, speaking for the first time since Mr. Barrow launched into his speech. His calm voice was laced with curiosity.

"Indeed, Lord Radnor. The theater company is based in New York City, which is growing bigger by the day. It's a city filled with energy, ambition, and opportunities for those good enough to seize them. I would sing its praises further, but I'm sure you know that already."

"And what would such an opportunity entail?" Dora asked. "Would she travel immediately? How long would she be expected to stay?"

"Ah, the practical questions," Mr. Barrow said with an amused chuckle. "If Lady Liana accepts, she'll be provided with quality accommodation and a stipend to cover her initial expenses as well as a generous salary. The contract would likely be for a year, with the option to extend if both parties are satisfied. Of course, the decision to extend or not rests entirely with her."

Liana's voice shook slightly as she spoke. "It's a generous offer, but I must admit the idea of leaving England ... leaving my family and loved ones ... is rather daunting."

Mr. Barrow nodded with a look of understanding. "I won't deny that such a choice requires courage. But consider this: opportunities like this are rare and often lead to growth beyond what we can imagine. I'm certain that your family would support you if you decided to leave for America. In addition, you'd have the chance to return as a celebrated singer, your name known on both sides of the Atlantic."

"I don't know what to say," she murmured, her gaze dropping to her hands.

"She'll think about it," Alex answered on her behalf. "This is an important decision, Mr. Barrow. Therefore, my sister requires ample time to ponder over it."

"That's correct," Gregory said, uttering his first words since the conversation about travelling abroad had begun. "Liana needs the space to gather her thoughts and get some more rest."

"You don't have to decide right away," Mr. Barrow told Liana gently. "Take some time to consider it. The offer will remain for quite a while."

"Thank you very much," Liana said, no longer feeling overwhelmed by the need to make a quick decision. "I'll be sure to do that." She snuck another glance in Gregory's direction, but his expression remained inscrutable.

"That's all I ask," Mr. Barrow replied with a warm smile. "Should you decide to accept, I have no doubt that you'll shine as bright and warm as the morning sun. You have all it takes to become a successful singer, after all."

"Thank you for visiting my sister, Mr. Barrow. It is always a delight to have you at Ravenmoore," Alex said, exchanging a handshake with the man.

"It is always a pleasure to be here," Mr. Barrow replied. He tipped his hat politely before exiting the room in his usual hurried manner.

"We should also leave. We have a lot to discuss," Alex said, moving toward the door. "Make sure to rest, Liana."

Gregory's eyes lingered on Liana briefly, with a warm look on his face that she recognized from the past.

"I wish you a quick recovery, Liana," he said to her in a tone that seemed surprisingly intimate. Before leaving the room, he turned to Dora. "And thank you for taking good care of her," he added before leaving the room. His presence was an impactful one, and the striking effect lingered after he was gone.

Liana missed his scent as soon as he shut the door quietly. The day had gone differently than she had imagined it would, and now there was a great deal more to consider. She took a deep breath and sank into the blanket mountain that had provided her with comfort all day.

"I wonder what decision you'll make," Dora said, "Of all of us three siblings, you're the one with the most interesting life currently. Leaving to become a singer in America would be frowned upon by society. Luckily, our family's influential enough to weather the gossip without negative outcomes."

"That's true," Liana mumbled, the bedding muffling her voice.

"Anyway, if you do decide to depart for America, we could go together. I'd paint all day, and you'd play in the best shows. Before we know it, we'll become the sensations of the century."

"That's quite an elaborate dream," Liana responded with some amusement.

Dora shrugged nonchalantly. "All I'm saying is, the idea of pursuing a musical line of work sounds good. And so does the idea of remaining in England. Each of those choices is equally valid."

Liana's gaze drifted to the window, where the sun rose high in the sky like a golden lamp. There was something beautiful about the way it stood out in the pale blue sky.

"Perhaps so," she responded softly, her thoughts drifting not to America, but to the man who had braved the storm to find her.

Chapter Eight

The next day was bright and sunny, rendering the cold from the stormy day into a mere memory. Liana had lounged in bed the previous day after her visitors left. She had given the offer proposed by Mr. Barrow some more thought, weighing his words in her mind. Now she was ready to leave the seclusion of her room and interact with the rest of the world.

The social affairs at the manor had gone smoothly in her absence. That spoke to Alex's organizational skills, with some aid from the housekeeper and Dora's capacity to spot and resolve little details. A picnic had been arranged for later that morning, an occasion for the guests to connect positively with one another and build lasting relationships.

After breakfast, guests began parading the gravel paths of the eastern garden, their laughter and conversation accompanying the chirping of birds. Light snacks and a lively array of games had been set out on high wooden tables. The seating arrangements were casual and left to individual choice, with quality chairs provided for the comfort of those who wished to sit and play games.

Liana found herself seated at one of the low wooden tables draped with lace and fine linens, her cup of tea replaced with lemonade served in delicate crystal glasses. Although the food had been set out so anyone could have their pick whenever they wished, well-dressed footmen busied themselves with serving the meals.

As the sun lazily shone down on them, the memories of the storm and all that accompanied pushed back to the surface. It was so strange and yet human, how one's circumstances could change in the blink of an eye. Previously, she was stuck in an unpleasant weather situation and on unfriendly terms with the man she cared most for in the world. Now she was seated comfortably on a nice, sunny day, and her relationship with Gregory had taken a positive turn.

They had finally bridged the barrier that had existed between them in those four years. Recalling how he'd come to check in on her the day before, Liana wondered if he would want to reignite their former romance. The possibility of the sweet love they had once shared blossoming again coaxed a tentative smile from her.

Across from her, Gregory pulled out a chair and sat. His sudden presence was impossible to ignore, and she met his gaze with a curious one of her own. Although his eyes held a guarded look as they had the previous day when he'd come to check on her, there was an unmistakable softness within their green depths.

"My lady," he said to her in that calming voice of his. "I was hoping you'd be out here."

"I decided the sunshine was much better to look at from the outdoors," she replied. "Splendid of you to join us."

"I couldn't resist the opportunity to play a few games," he said with a playful smile playing on his lips. "Would you like to play a game of Fox and Hound?"

"Why yes," she responded, recalling how they used to play the game on their many picnics together years ago. Gregory won most of the time, his strategic skills unrivaled by most.

Holding up a pair of carved wooden tokens that served as markers in the game, he turned to her with a smile. "Shall we begin?"

Liana picked her assigned pieces, ready to play. The game was simple enough, and the guests at Ravenmoore had taken a special liking to it during their stay. For added intrigue, each turn involved a small riddle or a clever challenge, and the victor would earn a point. The objective, of course, wasn't just victory. It was to tease and jest with one another in good fun.

"Very well then," Liana replied, her voice light with a tingle of something unspoken and warm. "But be warned, I have sharpened my wits since we last played together."

They began to play, Gregory's face in equal measures competitive and playfully teasing. Liana matched his stride, making strategic plays with a practiced hand. The last time they had played together, Gregory had won nearly all the rounds. His strategy had been difficult to spot—just when Liana thought she would win a round, she would be beaten awfully each time.

She hadn't consciously worked on it, but over the years, she had sharpened her wits. In this game, each round came with laughter and playful puzzles that were difficult to decipher. The world melted away, and soon all Liana could process was the gentle teasing from Gregory as their pieces traveled across the board. The emotional distance that had long kept them apart was being bridged, one smile and laugh at a time.

It almost seemed like they were the only ones in the garden, exchanging looks and teasing each other through a game that allowed them to communicate in the language of light-hearted competition.

"Answer this," Gregory began when it was his turn to tell a riddle. They were at the final stage, and her answer would determine who won the game. "I have cities, but no houses. Forests, but no trees. And water, but no fish. What am I?"

"A map," Liana said easily.

"I have been bested," Gregory said with laughter. "Congratulations on your victory."

Liana let out an unladylike whoop that would have been expected more from Dora, and that gesture only causes Gregory's laughter to deepen. She flashed him a dazzling smile, pure satisfaction written all over her face.

For a moment, their eyes met in silent connection and mutual respect. Yet, Liana felt a certain uneasiness at a new reservedness in Gregory's gaze. His eyes were still soft and affectionate, but there was also something secretive that made her uneasy. Just as she was about to ask, his voice broke the silence.

"It appears you've made proper use of our time spent apart," Gregory praised in a sincere tone of voice. "I never imagined that you would best me so effortlessly."

Her face burned pink at his praise. "While you were focused on conquering the world with your businesses, I busied myself with the little things."

"And succeeded on that front," Gregory added, his eyes never leaving hers. "You're a brilliant woman indeed."

Her blush deepened. She was thoroughly enjoying his praise and sweet demeanor. It was a delightful moment she did not want to end. A fleeting glimpse of the connection they once shared. She longed to have that again, and just as sentiment began to kindle and her heart fluttered in response, the moment abruptly ended.

Gregory glanced away, breaking the private hold they had shared. He was staring in another direction, and Liana followed his gaze.

Across the garden, a group of well-dressed ladies had gathered. Standing among them was Lady Emma. She was dressed in a deep blue gown that accentuated her poised elegance, and the air around her was clearly one of admiration and warm regard from the others.

Lady Emma made toward them with a radiant smile on her face. After they had exchanged greetings, she turned her attention toward Gregory.

"Mr. Holt, would you be so kind as to join us in the next activity? We would love to enjoy your pleasant company over there," she said, her tone suffused with charm and expectation.

For a moment, Gregory looked as if he intended to say no. As if he were reluctant to break the fragile intimacy budding between himself and Liana. Then the moment passed, and with a brief nod, he rose to his feet.

"I apologize for leaving abruptly," he said, offering Liana a fleeting smile that held some warmth and regret. "But it appears my attention is required elsewhere."

It was an odd sensation, but Liana felt incredibly alone as she sat at the table by herself. If it had been some other gentleman, she would not have minded his decision to excuse himself. Yet it felt painful that Gregory had chosen the company of another woman. They were not a couple, but she had held hope that he would realize his romantic feelings for her still lingered and they would start anew.

What did Gregory's decision to heed Lady Emma's invitation mean in the grand scheme of things? Could it be a mere polite gesture, or was it signaling something more? Perhaps she had been wrong to assume that Gregory and Lady Emma weren't romantically intertwined. Maybe he had just as much interest in her as she clearly did in him.

The thought stirred a painful pang in Liana's heart. She watched them go, her heart sinking further as the space between them widened and Gregory sat at another table with Lady Emma and her group.

As soon as he left, other people flocked to her table as though they had been awaiting their turn to play with her. She managed a smile as she picked up her token and began playing a game with a polite gentleman. And although she was present physically, her mind was elsewhere.

There was a chance that her understanding of their recent dynamic was wrong. She and Gregory had resolved their former conflict and were now on friendly terms. Maybe that was all there was to it. If he desired her in other ways than friendship, he had yet to prove it. She had been delusional to think there was something more.

The pang of hurt within her grew at an accelerated pace. Perhaps Gregory wanted only to be courteous to Lady Emma. After all, she had invited him politely, and they had been cordial for a while now at the estate. It would have been rude to turn her down.

The weight of her overthinking threatened to ruin what was otherwise a good day, so she resolved to stop. It was better to bury her disappointment and expectations instead of letting them consume her.

Liana directed her attention to the game at hand. The polite gentleman, Lord Gansey, had moved his pieces higher than was considered strategically smart, and now he was surrounded on all fronts.

"What will you do now?" she asked with forced cheer, determined to maintain a casual demeanor even as her heart was breaking.

"I must confess, I'm not as good at this game as I thought," Lord Gansey said, wiping a line of sweat from his brow.

"Allow me to do you a favor. I'll guide my pieces downwards so you have the chance to recover," she replied kindly.

Lord Gansey shot her a look filled with gratefulness and appreciation, which Liana accepted with a polite smile. It surprised her at times, how easily she could fit into society in moments when her inner life felt like it was in shambles.

The rest of the picnic activities passed by in a haze. Once, she glanced in Gregory's direction and saw that his attention was captured by a prolonged conversation with Lady Emma. The two seemed a perfect fit, equally good-looking and with a shared confidence that conquered any obstacle in their path.

As the picnic festivities drew to a close, the guests began to return to the manor. Some were preparing for an evening ride, and others had gone to have a nap before dinner. Liana went to a secluded corner of the garden. She was soon joined by Alex and Dora, who both seemed to have sensed that she was in a reflective state of mind.

The late afternoon sun bathed the flowers in a golden glow. The gentle murmurs of the remaining guests provided a soft backdrop to the loud thoughts in Liana's mind. Her eyes wandered, lost in thought of what was and what could be. Overwhelmed by her situation with Gregory and the uncertainties surrounding their current bond, she sighed softly.

"I must confess," she began. "Despite all that has happened, I've found that I remain deeply in love with Gregory."

Her voice trembled as she spoke, confessing her biggest secret to her siblings. She had always been the sort to manage her feelings privately, but the emotions within her only caused more words to tumble out rapidly.

"Yet, it seems utterly a foolish plan on my end to act on such sentiments, given the history between us. It seems only logical to let him move on and be happy, even if that happiness is found with another woman."

There was a brief moment of silence. Alex turned to her with a concerned look, his expression filled with tenderness and warmth. "Matters of the heart are rarely subject to logic, I'm afraid," he advised reasonably. "I imagine it's not easy to be in such a frustrating position. It seems that any decision you make is equally valid and invalidating."

"That may be true. However, I encourage you not to give up on the situation," Dora said. "Love isn't something to be abandoned at the first turn of adversity. You must not let the past dictate your future."

"That too is true," Alex said. "The final decision rests on you, Liana."

"Could you speak to Gregory on her behalf?" Dora asked earnestly. "Maybe even subtly threaten to—"

"I doubt a man like Gregory would take kindly to being threatened," Alex replied, his voice tinged with amusement.

Dora bit her lip. "That may be true. But even so, we can't let our little sister hurt like this."

"I know you're sympathetic to Liana's plight. Believe me, so am I. I desire to see her happily married and in a supportive relationship. But Liana is an adult, and so is Gregory. As a result, I consider it best not to interfere in these matters."

"You're both right," Liana said with a sigh. "It's my life and Gregory's. I just wish things didn't hurt as much as they do."

"I may not be able to interfere in your affairs, but I can ask Gregory to leave if his presence bothers you so," Alex offered kindly. "Say the word and I'll do it."

"Don't. I'm the one who needs to resolve my feelings, and I won't have him suffer for it."

"He would hardly be suffering," her brother responded. "As far as I know, all he wants to do is handle his duty here and return to London."

"No, don't," Liana repeated, shaking his head. "I do appreciate the offer, though."

Dora reached for Liana's hand and squeezed it with earnest conviction. "This may sound off from me, but it might be best to practice patience. You never know how things will turn out. We're here for you, dear sister, through every step of the way."

Liana's eyes glistened with tears as she processed her sister's words, her inner turmoil momentarily abated by her love for her family.

"Gregory isn't a man who can have his feelings easily swayed," she said with a sigh. "I suppose all I can do is wait and hope that everything turns out favorably."

Alex nodded in approval. "That's right, sweetheart. Gregory's path is his own. If his heart lies elsewhere, then you mustn't interfere. And if he wants you, he knows what to do. Do not burden yourself. You must care for yourself first."

Taking her siblings' advice into consideration, Liana was left with a bittersweet mix of hope and resignation. Alex and Dora's words had ignited a spark of determination within her. In that moment, she resolved to nurture her emotions and remain hopeful in the wake of everyday affairs.

* * *

At the other end of the Ravenmoore grounds, Gregory found himself wrestling with the events of the day. While he had entertained Lady Emma with affable charm and engaged in polite conversation with her group, his mind had wandered endlessly toward Liana. The softness in her eyes and her excitement at winning a round had reawakened a long-dormant buzz within him. He wanted to be next to her at all times, to soak in her words and relish the sound of her laughter. A persistent ache gnawed at him, a longing that he was familiar with. One that he refused to let cloud his better judgment.

Gregory excused himself from Lady Emma's table and moved further toward the left wing of the expansive garden, away from the crowd. He found a secluded bench beneath a grand elm tree and wasted no time in occupying it.

He enjoyed the peace and quiet, allowing his thoughts to wander freely. He couldn't help recalling the sweetness of Liana's smile as they played their game. There was also the brief yet precious connection that they shared before Lady Emma called him away.

All of that weakened his newly found resolve to keep his distance. He had intended to reignite their relationship before learning about Liana's chance at becoming a successful musician. If Mr. Barrow's invitation was appealing to her, he did not wish to be an obstacle complicating her decision. His feelings for her were fervent but, given the fact that she might be leaving for America soon, he didn't think it was best to make a move.

Gregory sighed deeply, plagued by his thoughts. He had even tried to publicly align himself with Lady Emma, in the hope that the restlessness in his heart would end. However, being away from Liana only made the agitation worse.

The idea of pursuing a different romance felt hollow when compared to the wonder of the bond he shared with Liana.

It would be best to scrap that plan altogether, Gregory thought. As long as he was on the estate, there was no point in courting another woman, because only Liana would remain in his mind.

Gregory's attention was abruptly drawn to a familiar figure moving across this line of vision. It was one of the footmen employed by the Foxworths, dressed in a distinctive blue uniform. The footman was carrying a meal platter, and there was something about his simple movements that seemed familiar. He frowned as he stared at the footman, unable to place why he stood out so much.

"Who is that man?" he asked a passing maid.

"T-that's Will, sir," the maid stammered out, clearly startled that she was being addressed directly. "He's a new employee at Ravenmoore. He has been working here for a few weeks."

Gregory thanked the maid and dismissed her. Before he could ponder his thoughts further, Alex joined him on the bench.

"Look who finally has the time to discuss necessary subjects," Gregory said dryly.

"Hosting duties are as unpleasant as they sound. I don't know why I do it," Alex replied.

"Because you're good at it."

"You're correct about that."

"In any case, we ought to move along with the business plan and make vital decisions," Gregory continued. "Time is a valuable asset on our side."

Alex nodded. "But first, are there any updates regarding that uncle of yours?"

"I received a letter from Russell, informing me that the old man has begun working hard to sabotage us," Gregory replied without missing a beat. He had shared the details of his family affairs with Alex since the start of their friendship, and the latter had expressed his support and sympathy over their plight. "That might include the planned manufacturing company."

"What an awful individual," Alex said distastefully.

Gregory sighed before nodding in agreement. "His machinations are designed to ruin my brother and me, preventing us from pursuing our ambitions and leaving us destitute."

"We had better act swiftly then. It's crucial that we secure our interests and speak with prospective investors before his shadow grows any longer."

"I intend to address the matter in court once proper evidence has been arranged. The sooner that happens, the sooner the issue can be put to rest," Gregory stated firmly. "However, my utmost priority is to begin working out the details of the business plan and speaking to prospective investors."

Alex offered a supportive smile. "My friend, we shall not let anyone jeopardize your future."

"That's a relief," Gregory said, sitting up straighter in his seat. "Now let us begin working on the business plan."

Chapter Nine

Liana's decision to remain patient in hopes that things would turn her way was met with direct opposition from the tides of fate. As the days passed, it grew increasingly difficult to catch a glimpse of Gregory. During two separate instances at breakfast, she had allowed herself a minute to glance around the dining hall in hopes of sighting him. A tall, broad-shouldered man like Gregory would be easy to spot, but her search yielded no results. It was clear that he wasn't present in the dining hall, or any other hall.

The situation felt like a reverse of the past when Gregory seemed to have endless time on his hands while she was busy with personal tutors. In those days, he would patiently wait outside her window until her lessons ended. Then they would discuss endlessly as the hours passed. Now he was a successful businessman who didn't need to report his movements to anyone before doing so.

Regardless of her concern, Liana was certain that he wouldn't just depart the estate abruptly. After all, he had come to Ravenmoore to fulfill his business purposes and would likely remain until that was resolved.

On the third day, she spotted him momentarily. His curly mass of hair drew her attention as he conversed quietly with Alex and a few other men. Before she could think or even call out to him, they disappeared into her brother's study for several hours. Her relief at seeing him was so great, she was filled with ample joy and energy.

Afterwards, Liana walked with a bounce in her step. The knowledge that he was present at the manor, albeit hidden, was exhilarating, and she allowed herself to dwell in the sensation. It was only hours later that she let the inevitable questions dance in her mind. Why was Gregory absent from social activities? Her only conclusion pointed to his business purposes. Perhaps he had decided it was time to get serious and accomplish his personal goals.

Still, a theory was incomparable to actual facts. What if her thoughts were wrong and he was unavailable for other reasons? Maybe he was in some trouble, or … Refusing to entertain more bad thoughts, Liana spoke with Alex, who validated her theory.

"Gregory's focused on drafting a profitable business plan," her brother explained with a smile. "I'm aware you miss him, but I assure you he's quite alright. The sooner he accomplishes this task, the better for us all."

Liana also discovered that Gregory had abandoned the dining hall for the private drawing room. It was there in the enclosed area that he took his meals, enjoying the tranquil environment before making his way back to his room without stopping for the occasional polite conversation.

During her rare glimpses of him, he often had a thoughtful and focused look on his face. Accompanying that was an air of strict determination. His striking smile was now overshadowed by eyebrows furrowed in confusion and a burning desire for success. In a way, it provided a perspective of him that she had never seen. It could not be denied that his self-discipline had played a huge role in his success.

She was proud of him, and yet she missed him greatly. Liana hoped that his efforts would result in positive results and that they could carry on as usual. His being absent made her realize she had participated in many of the arranged social events only because Gregory would be there. Otherwise, she'd be in her room poring over books or playing her dulcimer.

Since Gregory's new schedule showed no signs of change, she had begun to withdraw as well. She spent more time in the comfort of her room, watching the sky or playing a lovely tune on one of her musical instruments.

Dora joined her often, as if sensing that her retreat wasn't due to the guests, but because she missed Gregory's presence. Liana would listen and laugh as her sister shared the latest gossip and snippets about happenings around the estate, including details of who may marry whom by the end of summer.

On one such day, Liana sat quietly by the window with a book in hand. On the other side of the room, Dora was hard at work on a painting with fluid, deliberate strokes of her brush.

"It's such a bore. Working out the details of a business idea, I mean," Liana declared without turning, meaning to get Dora's attention. Her sister smiled and glanced up from her canvas.

"Well, I'd say it's only a bore for those waiting around. It is exhilarating, actually, thinking of a new idea, and fleshing it out to be profitable."

"How would you know?" Liana asked, turning to face Dora.

"I was unfortunate enough to have a similar experience with Alex, specifically when we were looking to expand the estate. A grueling process I would not want to undergo ever again," Dora noted with a brief frown before smiling once more. "Thankfully, we have enough wealth to last us multiple lifetimes. And with Alex's smart investments, we barely have financial troubles to worry about."

"I doubt that Gregory has financial troubles either, but you can't tell it with how focused he gets," Liana said.

That earned a laugh from Dora. "From what I have been told, Gregory is quite the intelligent man. His brain works wonders, and he's said to be exceptionally creative about business matters."

Liana blushed slightly at the praise doled out by her sister. She had always known Gregory was destined for great things. This was due to his refined way of thinking and his keen eye for spotting opportunities. It felt validating to hear someone else say the same thing.

"What's that?" Dora asked, making a pointing gesture with her paintbrush.

Liana blinked in confusion. "What do you mean?"

"That, on your gown," Dora replied, leaving her painting and covering the distance between them. She bent slightly to take a handful of Liana's satin fabric and examine it.

Following her sister's gaze, Liana spotted a delicately soft piece of apple fruit clinging to her gown. "I didn't know that was there."

"That much is obvious," Dora said with a brief eye roll. "Did you visit the kitchens? We didn't have fruit for breakfast today, or I might have attributed it to that."

"I can't say for certain how it got there," Liana said, dismissively brushing the fruit away. "You know how clumsy I can sometimes get."

"You aren't half as clumsy as Coral," Dora responded, referring to one of the maids. "One time, I witnessed her trip over her own feet. Some people are just less balanced, and there's nothing anyone can do about it."

"Coral makes up for her lack of balance with her talent for brewing delicious teas," Liana praised. "We can't all be good at everything."

"That's accurate," Dora said, nodding in agreement. "Take us, for example. I draw quite well, but if I ventured into singing, I'd send everyone off to the doctor with their ears bleeding."

"The same could be said for me. I can barely draw anything properly."

"On second thought, I suppose one can learn anything if one tries hard enough."

"Can I test that theory?" Liana asked, gesturing toward Dora's canvas. "I'll only make a few strokes with the brush." There was a playful twinkle in her eye as she waited, knowing how seriously Dora took her paintings.

"No, you may not," came Dora's prompt answer. And then the two sisters burst into amused laughter.

As she dwelt in the peaceful moment, Liana's thoughts drifted to a certain man. A man who seemed tethered to her in multiple ways. A man whom she had once lost and never wanted to be apart from again.

* * *

The afternoon sun was the warmest the Ravenmoore grounds had seen in almost a week. But that didn't stop the hunting activities and other outdoor events. Guests gathered in the garden to celebrate the birthday of an older gentleman of noble lineage. Liana intended to attend the event and not linger, but she had received a message from a maid informing her that Mr. Barrow had requested that she play during the celebration.

Since his earlier offer to take her to America and aid her in building a musical career, she had deliberately tried to keep their paths from crossing. That was because she was unsure of herself and had not yet arrived at a decision. She had everything she could want in England, but life in America seemed fresh and full of possibilities. Yet, at the same time, the notion of being away from her friends and family seemed lonely.

With the help of her lady's maid, she dressed in a pale yellow gown with a decent neckline. As she made her way into the garden, she flexed her finger in anticipation. After getting over her fear of performing in front of an audience, the prospect of playing the pianoforte or dulcimer publicly had become more appealing.

It would be nice if Gregory heard her play, she thought. Maybe the sound of her tunes filling the air would bring him out of his self-imposed retreat and provide her with a glimpse of his presence.

"Welcome, my lady," Mr. Barrow greeted as she stepped into the garden. "Are you ready to enthrall us with your talent?"

"Most certainly, Mr. Barrow," Liana replied, settling in the chair placed before the pianoforte. Her fingers hovered lazily over the keys as she examined her environment. The air was heavy with anticipation and the weight of expectant eyes. Some had heard her play previously and wished to experience it a second time. Then there were others who had gotten word of a lady with a flair for music and wished to witness it themselves.

Liana pressed down on the keys with a deliberate fluidity at first. And then, as if compelled by the music itself, her fingers moved instinctively and she got lost in the tunes. The world melted away, and she became one with the sweet melody. She was transported to a different space, one where she didn't have to worry about a potential musical career or her complicated relationship with Gregory.

"That was splendid!" Mr. Barrow cried out after the final note had melodiously eased into nothingness. He clapped his hands together, clearly enchanted by what he had just listened to.

The entire room joined him in a resounding applause. Liana blushed and glanced down shyly. When she felt comfortable enough to raise her head, her eyes scanned the crowd quickly for a particular figure whom she hoped had caught her performance.

"Lady Liana, you are indeed magnificent," Mr. Barrow exclaimed as they joined Dora, who was waiting by the side with a proud smile on her face. "I truly hope that you will consider my offer to come to America and explore your magnificent talent. Trust me, you'll be a sensation to behold—one that kings, merchants, and lords would travel long distances to watch."

Liana glanced at the floor. "Mr. Barrow, I—"

"I appreciate your earnestness, Mr. Barrow, but you ought to let Liana ponder the decision on her own," Dora interrupted, stepping in on her behalf. "As you well know, a decision such as this cannot be made lightly. Thankfully, the Foxworths aren't a family easily influenced by societal expectations. That means we'll consider your offer, instead of rejecting the notion outright. Aristocrats like ourselves tend to frown against working for monetary gain."

Mr. Barrow looked chastened. It was clear that he was only being enthusiastic and meant no harm. "That's quite true, my lady. I deeply apologize for making you feel pressured."

"That's alright, Mr. Barrow," Dora said sweetly. "I know you only have Liana's best interests at heart."

"I am grateful for that as well," Liana added.

Barrow gave a nod of satisfaction. "Well, I must leave now. I hope everything turns out well in the end."

After a polite bow, Mr. Barrow joined the crowd and the celebrations. Liana and Dora ventured away from the crowd, choosing to settle on a bench nearby.

"What are you thinking, Liana?" Dora asked softly.

"I'm not quite sure," she replied honestly.

She had always lived a simple life and had been resigned to things remaining that way until she met Gregory. His arrival was like a bright star signaling alternate paths to explore. He had encouraged her to pursue her interests and expressed his love for her passionately.

In taking up Mr. Barrow's offer, she'd be exploring a different way of living and meeting new people. The idea of fame and a life replete with art, passion, and the adoration of an appreciative audience sounded nice, but it certainly wasn't worth being so far away from Gregory and potentially losing him again.

"I'll be in support of you, no matter what you decide," Dora reassured with an encouraging smile.

Liana returned the smile before sighing deeply. "It's just … I've never had to make a decision like this before."

Her heart lurched with apprehensive thoughts concerning risking her present situation with Gregory. Going away when the gap that formerly existed between them was in the process of being bridged seemed like a terrible decision. The hungry void within her was more likely to be filled by love and adoration from Gregory, not by fame.

The sound of guests chatting and laughing, along with chirping birds, filled the air around them.

Liana was pulled from her thoughts as Dora reached for her hand, squeezing gently. "In all of this, you must consider what makes you happy. If the path to fulfilment lies in embracing your talent on a broader stage, then perhaps it is worth leaving England for. There's also Mr. Holt to consider … he may be distant now, but I have seen the love in his eyes. The future holds much promise for you two."

Liana felt a pleasant flush of warmth in response to her sister's words. She had grown more uncertain in recent days as Gregory grew occupied with his tasks. Although she told herself the situation had nothing to do with her—after all, he had his own reasons for traveling down to Ravenmoore Estate—a minor part of her brain argued that it was unlikely that he would ever care for her romantically again.

After all, he had chosen Lady Emma's company over hers without a second thought. He also hadn't made attempts to seek her attention since their last conversation.

"I truly hope you're right, Dora. Given the way his mind has been set on business matters, I am scared that there's no room in his heart for me anymore."

"Don't say that," Dora responded in a resolute tone. "His reasons for being slow and hesitant are perfectly understandable. The first relationship you two shared ended terribly. I'm certain his feelings for you still hold strong, only this time he's trying to be cautious. We can't blame him for it, can we?"

"You're absolutely correct. We can't, indeed," Liana said. In situations like this, it helped to have someone she trusted by her side. Someone who could analyze situations with a clear head as Dora did.

"I'm never wrong about these things," Dora declared before continuing, "Liana, the man braved a storm to find you! And when you two played the Fox and the Hound, he laughed the hardest I have ever seen."

"I don't wish to lose him again," Liana whispered. "I sound pathetic, don't I? The pitiful heroine waiting around for the undecided hero instead of taking up a life-changing offer."

"You're a lot of things, my dear, but never pitiful," her sister responded, drawing closer for a hug. "Never that."

Chapter Ten

Starting a new business was no easy feat and required great planning before execution. In the case of a manufacturing company, an important consideration was raising capital through one's social network and valued partnerships. In addition, necessary resources would need to be sourced, and the premises for the factories had to be identified. Many businessmen considered the decision-making process a tiring task, but for Gregory, such enterprises were a welcome challenge. He enjoyed the process of strategizing and mapping out the different branches of a new project.

That was why he had succeeded greatly as a businessman where many others had failed. At Ravenmoore, there was a diverse arrangement of businessmen whom he could consult on ideas. Alex was one such man, and, after a few days of planning and reviewing, they had arrived at a brilliant plan that would certainly set their new business up for success.

The first factory would be built in the heart of London, in an efficient location that was close to a skilled labor force and a railway station. Once titles to the land were secured, the construction plans would begin. Radnor's influence had allowed for beneficial legal agreements to be quickly drawn up and signed.

Everything was in perfect alignment, just the way Gregory liked it. The days he'd spent pondering and planning had proven successful. The only part he hadn't factored in was how much he'd found himself missing Liana.

Increasingly, his feelings had made themselves difficult to ignore. Even as his thoughts were occupied by engineering and business concepts, she had managed to appear regularly in his mind.

He'd found himself wondering what she was doing and if she'd cared enough about his absence to enquire about it. Late into the nights as he examined architectural plans for the new factories, a familiar whiff or sound would remind him of Liana. Memories of her filled his dreams, floating in tandem with the sound of her laughter. It was pure, undiluted torture.

The only thing that kept him from acting on his strong feelings were the tasks he busied himself with and the harsh prospect that Liana would be leaving the country soon. He would never be so selfish as to ask her not to pursue her dreams for his sake. Therefore, it was best to keep his distance. No matter how painful that felt.

After a long meeting with Alex spent smoothing over the final pieces of their business plan, Gregory emerged from the study with his face glowing with excitement. The manufacturing company was undoubtedly going to be a success, resulting in more freedom from pointless entanglements with his uncle.

Alex joined him, and together the two men walked along the hallway.

"Triumph looks good on you, friend," the earl commented. He was a man who liked doling out praise when needed.

"It'll look even better when the processes are underway," Gregory replied. "Moreover, I have you to thank for all this progress."

"I've had the experience of working with many men, but, as always, collaborating with you leads to prominent and remarkable results," Alex insisted, slapping his shoulder in a friendly gesture.

Gregory returned the gesture with one of his own. "I can only hope that fortune continues to smile upon us. This is a new phase of something we'll be running together for quite a long time. We're both disciplined men, and I predict that we'll have tangible results before long."

"We most certainly will," the earl said in agreement. Beyond their business unions and other situations, their friendship was a priority for both. "I have arranged a ball to celebrate this achievement of ours, and it will be held this evening. I encourage you to attend and bring a partner along."

"This evening?" Gregory asked with a raised eyebrow. "That is incredibly short notice."

Alex had the decency to look momentarily sheepish. "I had intended for it to be a surprise, actually. An evening of socializing is precisely what you need after being secluded from the public for days on end."

"I suppose you're right," Gregory replied. "It would serve me well to experience the harmonious lull of a social event again. I already know the ball will not be boring. Your hosting skills are unmatched."

"Correct. I shall leave you to prepare for the ball," Alex said before pivoting in another direction.

Gregory continued his trip through the hallways to his private quarters, his mind wandering down a path of bittersweet introspection. He wondered if Liana was preparing for the upcoming ball, making final decisions about her outfit alongside other decisions ladies tended to make. The answer was likely yes. She was a part of the hosting family, after all, and would have little reason to miss such an event.

Thinking of her made his heart ache. They had come so far in recent weeks, having gone from two people with a shared history that separated them to individuals who now had a rapidly budding bond. Images of her flew through his mind. The memory of her gentle smile, the way her eyes held his in peaceful harmony. He longed to tell her about the recent breakthrough and how he was gaining more power against his uncle's meddling nature. Being away from her had only caused him to miss her more greatly.

However, seeing her now would only bring him torture. Knowing she'd be as dazzling and enchanting as always, yet inaccessible for him to express his through to fully. If she did decide to move to America, they would see each other even less. She'd be preoccupied with her new life, her senses taken in by new experiences.

He should be happy for her, Gregory thought with a bittersweet feeling. After all, he'd always encouraged her to follow her passions and live true to herself. He'd sooner jump in a lake of fire than attempt to derail her dreams.

A trip to London was beyond due. Perhaps what he needed was to settle his affairs and depart from Ravenmoore. Then, in the comfort of his townhouse, he would ponder his thoughts with a calm mind and take charge of what needed to be done. That was a much better option compared to daydreaming about Liana and pining hopelessly for her.

There was a level of irony involved in the entire situation. Whereas upon arriving in Ravenmoore Estate, he had held certain resentments against Liana and frankly wished to have little or no conversation with her, the reverse had occurred. Now he was the one thinking about her all the time and restraining himself from seeking her out. Similarly, she'd let him go once so he could attain success. Now he was doing the same, keeping his distance so she could pursue her dreams. It was ironic to say the least.

Gregory sighed and tucked his hands into his pockets, his thoughts drifting to a recurring event over the previous nights. Every evening, a maid would knock and present him with a cup of freshly squeezed fruit juice. It was a refreshing drink, with an aroma so delightful he found himself looking forward to it at the end of the day. It was a blend of berries and citrus in equal measure, stirred finely and filled with flavors he loved the most.

Was it a coincidence that the drink being delivered was one of his favorites? Alex might have ordered the creation of the drink, but there was no way he knew the flavors Gregory preferred. The only person who knew how much he loved fruits was Liana. Was she the one sending the drinks? And if so, why? There was also a chance that this was all a coincidence.

Alex had told him to bring a partner along to the ball. He was going to ask Liana, Gregory decided. It was the least he could do to make up for his unexplained disappearance, and moreover, the evening would be better spent in her company. Also, he could ask her about the fruit drink and dispel any confusion.

"Mr. Holt! I'm beyond pleased to have found you," Lady Emma exclaimed, stepping into his path. "I understand that you have been occupied by pressing business matters."

"Correct, my lady," Gregory responded.

"I hope you'll accept my felicitations on your recent breakthrough."

He smiled gratefully. "Most certainly. Thank you for taking the time to do so."

"I trust you're prepared for tonight's festivities?" Lady Emma inquired, her tone imbued with a warmth that contrasted with the turmoil of his thoughts.

"I suppose one must be. After all, the earl did say it was being held in my honor. In fact, I look forward to participating in the revelry after a few days of serious work."

"Lovely. Like you, I'm someone who understands the value of setting goals and working hard to achieve them. But I also do appreciate spending time with others, enjoying favors provided by society."

Gregory nodded. "We're rather alike in that aspect."

"I do not wish to bore you, therefore I shall leave you to be on your way. Before I go, may I intrude upon your contemplation with a small proposal?"

He raised a curious eyebrow. "A proposal?"

"Indeed. At first, I considered playing the role of the patient, demure lady who waits to receive an invite," Lady Emma confessed. "But I'm afraid I possess not such patience. Therefore, I have decided to pose the question myself. I was wondering if you might consider being my dance partner for the ball tonight."

For a long moment, Gregory's mind raced as he considered the request. His utmost desire was to attend the ball with Liana, but that was probably a terrible idea, given his decision to refrain from acting romantically so she could arrive at a decision concerning her future without undue influence. Going with Lady Emma was a more sensible choice. She was a charming and agreeable lady who deserved to find requited love.

Now that his affections for Liana were undeniable, it would be unfair to keep indulging Lady Emma's attention. Accepting her partnership invitation was the least he could do before informing her he did not entertain a matrimonial interest in her.

Gregory hesitated, clearing his throat. "Lady Emma, you must forgive me if I seem a little distracted," he paused, weighing his words before continuing, "I shall be honored to dance with you this evening."

Lady Emma smiled broadly, her eyes lighting up. "Splendid! I believe we shall have an evening filled with wonderful delight and merriment."

Although her tone was playful, there was clearly an undercurrent of expectation lying beneath it. A silent hope that his acceptance was a sign of something more than mere courtesy.

Gregory was certain he didn't like Lady Emma in a romantic manner. However, she was an incredibly graceful and agreeable lady who would make a perfect wife for a different gentleman, and he wished her happiness.

He felt a pang of guilt as he spoke. "I must confess that I have some news to share later tonight," he said, searching her face for any revealing information. There was none, so he continued, "Yet I will accept your request. But I urge you not to think too highly of my actions."

Lady Emma nodded as though she understood his inner conflict more than he would ever care to reveal to her. "Very well, Mr. Holt. I appreciate your candor."

Just then, a maid carrying a tray of his refreshing fruit drink passed by, heading predictably in the direction of his room. The cool scent of berries and citrus filled the air pleasantly.

"That smells heavenly, doesn't it?" Lady Emma said, breathing in the scent.

"It does, indeed," Gregory replied in agreement. His attempts to ask the maids for more information had resulted in no response. Clearly, whoever had asked for the drinks to be delivered didn't wish for their gesture to be dwelt upon.

"I shall hereby take my leave. I'll see you soon!" Lady Emma said before taking a different path.

Gregory arrived at his bedroom with no further interruption and wasted no time in getting dressed for polite company. He made final adjustments to the collar of his tailcoat before making his way toward the grand ballroom.

The music was slow and subdued, a sign that the ball hadn't yet begun, and guests poured in through the entrance in their remarkable outfits. The sound of soft laughter and murmured greetings imbued with excitement filled the hallways.

Moving among the refined laughs and swirling gowns, he tried to push thoughts of Liana away. Yet, his eyes found themselves momentarily scanning the room, hoping to get a glance of her radiating beauty and lose himself in it.

As the host, Alex was already in the ballroom, greeting and entertaining his guests. He approached Gregory and acknowledged his outfit with a look of appraisal.

"That's a splendid suit, if I have ever seen any."

"It's Coltoú. One of the newest editions," Gregory replied. Coltoú was an international clothing company renowned for its quality coats.

"It's a worthy purchase," Alex noted. "You seem burdened by some concerns I cannot decipher. I assumed this must be due to the worry about our business venture. We have made headway, and yet you're as pale as a ghost."

Gregory swirled the glass of wine in his hand and glanced around the ballroom, unconsciously searching for Liana again.

"Radnor," he said quietly, leaning closer to avoid being heard by others. "Do you think it foolish to still be haunted by thoughts of a woman with whom a future looks uncertain?"

The earl regarded him thoughtfully, knowing fully well who the woman in question was.

"Foolish perhaps," he replied slowly. "That part is debatable and dependent on the individual. The heart is not always governed by logic, my dear friend. Sometimes, what seems like the futility of a future is merely the persistence of true emotion enveloped in the inability of the party to properly express themselves."

Gregory sighed with heavy resignation. "I have attempted to forget her, to move on ... yet each time I see her smile or hear her gentle laughter, I am reminded that it is her I truly want."

Alex listened diligently before placing a firm hand on his shoulder. "Then perhaps the only wisdom is in acknowledging that truth and learning to live with it until circumstances change or you carve a beneficial path without waiting around."

"Carve a path? There's a chance that it would be futile or foolish."

"Well, it's considerably more foolish to pine in agony forever," Alex replied with a supportive pat before walking away to welcome a few guests who were making their way into the ballroom.

Chapter Eleven

The excitement of the ball preparations had transformed the corridors of Ravenmoore Estate into a whirlwind of delicate activity. By evening, Liana found herself alongside the flurry of servants and attendants, providing the final touches in the grand ballroom. Silk fabrics had been draped over towering columns, crystal chandeliers were polished until they shone like captured starlight, and fragrant bouquets were arranged meticulously on every table. Yet beneath the surface of those busy tasks, Liana's heart lay heavy with conflicting feelings.

After aiding the staff in making vital design choices, Liana made her way to her bedchamber to get dressed. Unbidden, thoughts about Gregory came to her mind. A flash of his smile, a relic from her memories, ushered a wave of positive emotions within her. No doubt, he was also getting ready in anticipation of the evening activities. It was a shame that the ball was being organized so last-minute. Left to her, she'd have ensured that Gregory got enough rest in his quarters before having to socialize, which tended to be an exhausting activity.

Regardless, she was looking forward to seeing and speaking to him again. Once the ball unfolded fully in its genteel splendor, she was going to muster up enough courage to ask him to dance. It had to be a simple request. Nothing overly emotional or verbose. She had no desire to frighten Gregory off or complicate their situation further. It would merely be a chance to enjoy themselves and converse. He was likely still a skilled dancer, perhaps even better than he had been four years ago. In the past, she had always appreciated how easily he guided her along the dance floor and his gentle touch on her hand as they swayed in rhythm to the music.

She spotted a cluster of elegantly dressed ladies in the hallway, all chattering excitedly. Lady Emma stood at the center of attention, her eyes glimmering with excitement as she regaled the group with what seemed like an exciting story. Upon overhearing the name "Mr. Holt," Liana's interest was piqued. She drew closer, hoping to catch the story as well, when Lady Emma caught sight of her.

"Ah, our hostess has shown up," Lady Emma said in a friendly tone. "We were engrossed in conversation, when we should be in attendance at the ball. Have you come to call on us?"

"Not at all," Liana replied. "The ball is yet to begin, but you're right. The guests ought to be taking their positions at the moment."

"In that case, it would be foolish to delay further and show up late," Lady Emma remarked. "Come, ladies. We had best visit the ballroom before it becomes unfashionable to enter."

Giggling and muttering in agreement, the ladies began to make their way toward the ballroom.

"Actually, might I have a second with you, Lady Emma?"

"Most certainly," the lady in question replied. "What is it that you'd like to discuss?"

Liana had to admit that a lady like Lady Emma was impossible to dislike. Not only was she kind and easygoing, she had a practiced charm that endeared others greatly.

"I happened to hear you say something about Mr. Holt. Could you please repeat that?"

Lady Emma raised a quizzical eyebrow, but thankfully didn't make any questioning statements. Her lips formed into a proud smile as she replied, "I was informing the other ladies about my partner for the ball. He's none other than Mr. Holt, a gentleman whose attention I have come to appreciate."

Liana felt as though the wind had been knocked out of her. Things were already strange, and now they fell into the realm of shocking. Maybe she was wrong about everything. About Gregory's feelings ... about what the future held for them. It was clear that she was being delusional about the bond they shared, and he'd already moved on with someone else.

Dora was wrong, Liana thought. He wasn't trying to be cautious because he feared a repeat of their first relationship. He simply didn't care to seek her attention or raise her expectations. She'd been wrong to think he was away due to his business priorities. That was certainly a key reason, but perhaps he had also kept his distance on purpose—to express his disinterest in rekindling a romantic relationship—and she'd been too ignorant, too fanciful to realize it.

"Thank you for the information," Liana replied. "I am so happy for you, Lady Emma, and I hope you have an enjoyable night."

"I hope you do too!" Lady Emma responded.

Liana continued in the direction of her bedroom, her mind reeling with what seemed like a thousand thoughts. She'd been stupid to dwell on Gregory when his feelings for her were nothing close to what she felt. There was no point in spending time thinking about him, talking about him with her siblings, or considering him in her future plans. The only logical thing to do was to stay back and let him be happy with Lady Emma.

The mental image of the two twirling together in effortless harmony and grace stung her with a fresh sense of abandonment. They did make a good pair, Liana thought painfully. Lady Emma was graceful with an incredibly bright aura, and Gregory was a sight to behold, in addition to being successful.

They were no longer bright-eyed young adults with endlessly high hopes for the future. She'd been foolish to think she ever stood a chance to be the romantic partner to his fully realized self.

With the assistance of a maid, Liana got dressed in a splendid ball gown that was a shade of blue so pale it looked white at first glance. She had hoped that the night would be filled with many positives, but that seemed to no longer be a possibility. Now she had to prepare herself to see Gregory waltzing with Lady Emma in the ballroom.

She'd looked forward to tonight, hoping to dance under the shiny glamor of the lights with the man she loved. She'd picked out her gown, excited to exude elegance and reignite the flames that had burned into existence on the day they met four years ago. It seemed futile to dwell on those details, especially when he was already attending with Lady Emma.

She stood before the grand mirror in her room, carefully securing the last braid in her intricate updo. The light blue gown she wore caught the light and shimmered, its brocade fabric hugging her form with deliberate elegance. A beaded ribbon was woven carefully through the braids, each piece polished so brightly it shone. Soft curls framed her face, highlighting her fine features. She adjusted the delicate gold chain at her throat, the embedded pearl pendant resting just above her collarbone in a brilliant design.

Dora entered the room, her face lighting up as she registered Liana's entire outfit.

"You look like a dream," she remarked, watching as Liana smoothed her gloves, the soft fabric forming around her fingers effortlessly. "I daresay Mr. Holt will have no choice but to stare."

Liana sighed deeply, fastening a bracelet around her wrist. "And yet, it matters little, doesn't it? He's already found a partner for the evening."

Dora arched an eyebrow, undeterred. "A partner for the ball, yes. But a partner for his heart? I highly doubt it."

Liana turned from the mirror, her expression a mix of longing and resignation. "He's made his choice, Dora. Lady Emma is a perfect match for him. She's charming, well-connected, and entirely suited to his ambitions. And if not her, someone who isn't as insensible and timid as myself would be equally befitting," she finished, a defeated look etched on her face.

Dora sat on the chaise, rolling her eyes. "Oh, spare me your tragic monologue. You are neither weak nor foolish, Liana. And Gregory Holt, well, he may be clever in business, but when it comes to love, he is as blind as a kitten. If you want him, you must stop assuming the worst."

Liana offered a tiny, rueful smile. "And what do you suggest? That I march up to him and demand he see me the way he once did?"

Dora grinned. "That would certainly be amusing. But no, dear sister. I simply mean you should not surrender to doubt so quickly. Let him see you, really see you. If he's as lost as you claim, then so be it. But if there's a flicker of what once was ... then he'll show it through his actions."

Liana turned to the mirror, fingers grazing the cool pearl at her throat. Could she really bring herself to hope? Or was she only prolonging the inevitable heartache?

A soft knock on the door signaled that it was time. She took a steadying breath, gathering the folds of her gown. Whatever the night held, she would meet it with grace. And if Gregory had truly moved on, she would find the strength to do the same and finally let him go.

As she descended the grand staircase into the golden-lit ballroom, she prepared herself for any outcome. At their entrance, the ballroom went still, and every eye went to Liana and Dora. That was to be expected, given that they were a part of the family hosting the ball. Although her usual shyness loomed beneath the surface, Liana reminded herself to hold her head high and walk with grace.

By random chance, her eyes roamed the room briefly and landed on Gregory. He looked ... smitten by her, but there was also a hint of something else hidden beneath those green eyes of his. Unsure of what it meant, she glanced away and diverted her attention to her steps. It would be tragic to trip or miss her step in such a moment.

As they joined the crowd, a gentleman approached Dora. "May I have this dance?"

"Most certainly," Dora replied, allowing him to take her hand and guide her toward the dance floor.

The room had come alive with movement, guests in exquisite attire gliding gracefully across the polished floor. Liana lingered at the edge of the crowd, her gaze drifting over the dancing couples with a mixture of wistfulness and resignation. The ball had once been a beacon of hope for her. Now it seemed to underscore the widening gulf between her heart and the man she still loved.

She caught a glimpse of Gregory and Lady Emma, the two spinning in a skillful style on the dance floor. They made a fine pair, she thought with a painful pang.

Amid the swirling dancers and the soft strains of the orchestra, Lord Gansey, the gentleman with whom she'd played a game of the Fox and the Hound, approached her with an earnest look on his face.

"Lady Liana," he began, bowing slightly. "May I have the pleasure of a dance?"

Liana considered his offer. Her heart was too heavy to entertain any attention, but she did not wish to appear ungracious to a gentleman who had been nothing but kind to her.

"Thank you. It would be my pleasure," she replied softly, taking his offered hand.

"I must admit, I hold you in high regard, Lady Liana," Lord Gansey confessed, his face glowing red. "You're as beautiful and well-mannered as I have imagined."

Lord Gansey was a young gentleman with a decent inheritance and a farmland he was due to inherit upon his father's death. His eyes were gentle and his smile was tentative without being insincere. He was by no means a handsome man, but his plain features had an endearing quality to them.

This was the kind of man she should naturally come to love, Liana thought. And she might have, if she hadn't met Gregory on that fateful day four years ago. Men like Lord Gansey were rather straightforward, their interests were predictable, and their lifestyle was constant. There would be no sudden journeys to Brazil or well-conceived plans for a profitable company.

Lord Gansey was a titled gentleman who held labor in contempt. Instead, he relied on the regular allowances from his family's estate and enjoyed the benefits his title accrued to him. If they got married, their life together would be boring and unremarkable, but it would at least be devoid of chaos and confusion.

It was too bad she couldn't fall in love with him, Liana thought with an internal sigh. He deserved better than to be compared constantly with Gregory in her mind.

"Thank you for your kind words, Lord Gansey," she replied.

In accordance with the musical cues, they entered the dance floor, the soft strains of a quadrille guiding them through graceful turns and measured steps. Liana followed Lord Gansey's lead as their movements lined up in smooth but impersonal steps.

She forced a polite smile, nodding as he commented on the evening's finery. He was an earnest man who often had the habit of speaking for extended periods about subjects relating to the parliament. Although Liana listened without complaint, she had to admit that it was difficult to maintain an interest in the conversation. Also, her mind and body were attuned to something else.

Gregory was standing a few steps away, and, without looking, she could tell exactly how close he was. A strange awareness tugged at her, pulling her attention towards him like an invisible force. There was a shift in the quadrille formation, and the partners changed. Mindlessly following the rhythm, she turned and found herself face to face with Gregory.

For a brief, breathless second, neither of them moved. The dance had dictated the moment, but fate seemed to have conspired to make it something else entirely. The noise in her head quieted down as his green eyes burned into hers, filled with something warm and hard to identify. Her breath caught as he took her hand, his grip first yet reverent, as though he had been waiting for her ... for this ... all night.

His eyes searched hers for some kind of answer as they began to move along to the music. This was no longer just a dance; it was a conversation without words. A whisper filled with promises of the longing they felt, woven into each step.

The energy between them radiated as her steps perfectly matched his. The touch of his fingers on her waist sent warmth through her veins. She tried to steady her breath, to maintain some detachment, but he was too close, too overwhelming. When she'd hoped to have a dance with him tonight, she had no idea it would happen like this and certainly never thought it would be so torturous.

Gregory tilted his head slightly, his voice just above a whisper. "You look breathtaking."

Liana swallowed, trying to summon something clever in response, but her voice betrayed her. All she could manage was an audible, deeply felt sigh.

His fingers brushed against hers, a fleeting touch but devastating in impact. She steeled herself against the touch and watched as surprise flashed briefly through his eyes. They spun again, and for one excruciating moment she was pressed against him, caught in the heat of the moment.

She lifted her eyes to meet his and was surprised to find the soft gaze on his face. He cared for her. In that moment, that much was undeniable. The realization was relieving and confusing at the same time.

Before she could dwell on it, the music shifted, signaling a change in partners. Gregory hesitated visibly, and in a split second that was barely long enough for her to feel the loss of him, he let her go, and she found herself again in Lord Gansey's arms.

The electrifying moment was gone, yet her body still trembled with the ghost of his touch.

In her current state, she could barely last another dance session. She turned to leave Lord Gansey with an apologetic smile.

"My Lord, I believe I need some air," she said, attempting to mask her shaky voice.

Ever the gentleman, Lord Gansey nodded and inclined his head. "Shall I escort you?"

"No, thank you. I only need a moment," she responded, slipping away from his hold and out of the ballroom. As she walked, she could feel her heart pounding like war drums in her chest.

Did Gregory love her?

Or was he toying with her heart?

She had no idea. The only thing she was certain of was the strong awareness that she needed to escape the ballroom before she lost herself completely.

Chapter Twelve

Gregory had watched as Liana descended the stairs into the grand ballroom with Dora, and he couldn't help staring intensely at her. She'd looked absolutely breathtaking, her hair and clothing aligning in a perfect match. He'd watched her linger at the edge of the crowd before being asked by Lord Gansey to dance. Then she'd joined everyone else on the dance floor, and it had taken Gregory everything in him to resist the urge to call out her name with as much passion as he felt.

As he danced with Lady Emma, he'd found his eyes drawn to Liana. It was as though the woman he was with didn't exist at all, because only Liana occupied his mind. Then she was in his arms, and he'd felt a strong urge to hold her all night, never letting go. She felt as delicate and special as antique china. So exquisite. Her scent was a mixture of lavender and rose, intoxicating his senses.

And even now, as he spun along the dance floor with Lady Emma, he could not remove her scent from his mind. He'd watched her leave the room, as the knowledge that their brief moment must have shaken her intensely revealed itself to him. It would be unfair to let her go without answering her unspoken questions. This was his time to act.

The dance came to a natural stop, and Gregory led Lady Emma to a quiet alcove in the ballroom.

"Lady Emma," Gregory started firmly. "I must speak with you for a moment."

His tone was measured, and, although he smiled kindly, there was an undercurrent beneath his words that likely provided an inkling of what he was going to say.

"Most certainly, Mr. Holt. What is it that troubles you?" she asked, concerned by the serious look on his face.

"I have been thinking a great deal about our present arrangement. While I appreciate the kindness of your company over the past few weeks, I fear that what we share can never transcend beyond friendship. I fear that is all I can ever offer at this time and in future."

Lady Emma absorbed his words with a look of understanding. "I understand that," she said quietly. "It's rather important to be honest with oneself and those who care for us. If friendship is what you can offer, then I shall treasure it as much as any other affection."

Before he could thank her, she asked with a refined boldness. "May I ask this ... are you still in love with Miss Foxworth?"

Her question was laced with curiosity, but the directness of it was unexpected. Gregory's eyes darkened as he pondered which to choose: confession or concealment. In the end, he decided on confession and began to respond.

"It would be a lie to say that my heart is entirely free of her memory. I yearn for her constantly, so much so that it is sometimes unbearable. At the moment, we're building a different kind of relationship, which may not ignite the same flames as before, but offers a different kind of solace."

He paused, taking a brief break to gather his thoughts. "I miss the intense, awe-filled look she unknowingly gave me. I miss being next to her, knowing that was all I needed to be spurred to improve myself. However, our current circumstances require clear thinking and sound judgment."

Lady Emma inclined her head in prompt acceptance. "Then let us be friends, Mr. Holt. Your heart clearly belongs to another. Time will reveal our true inclinations"

The conversation ended with a clear, unspoken understanding of a mutual agreement between them. Afterwards, Gregory realized he couldn't stay in the grand ballroom any longer. He had to find Liana in that instant. With a hasty goodbye directed at Lady Emma, he left the ballroom in pursuit of the woman he adored.

She was seated beneath a sprawling oak tree in the garden, the cool night air teasing a few strands from her coiffure. The air carried the faint scent of lavender and rose, intermixed with damp earth from a brief rainfall that had occurred earlier in the day.

Liana's scent, the lavender and rose, which had nearly driven him insane all evening, now held him in close proximity. It held a promise of many things: love, a happy future together, and so much more.

The manor buzzed with activity, quite different from the quiet garden. There was hearty laughter from the guests, and music spilled from the ground floor, where people waltzed hand to hand in accordance with melodious musical notes. In the garden, crickets chirped regularly, and the moon cast its silver glow over the earth.

Liana turned away from the entrance and stared into the darkness ahead as though lost in it.

Gregory's heart still pounded with the memory of their dance. Every step had felt like a silent battle, a test of wills. Several unaddressed feelings were lurking at the forefront, echoed in every movement. He'd felt it as he took her hand, feeling the soft press of her palm against his as they moved in perfect, agonizing synchrony. He'd felt as though this was something he needed desperately, and yet there was a sheer discomfort about the tension between them.

Shaking the thought from his mind, Gregory drew closer and touched Liana's shoulder lightly. She stiffened at the unexpected touch, but once she turned around and realized it was him, a look of surprise crossed her riveting features.

"I see you're enjoying the cool atmosphere. You've always had a talent for identifying rare and beautiful moments."

"Oh, I ..." She glanced down at her interlaced fingers and swallowed before continuing. "I needed this, actually. Needed to be out here because I was afraid I would lose myself."

Without waiting around for an invitation, Gregory sat beside her, simultaneously loosening his cravat for added comfort. "Why?"

"Hm?" Liana asked, blinking in confusion.

"Why were you afraid?" He clarified, shooting her a look of interest as he awaited her response.

For a moment, Liana looked as though she might respond, then with a casual purse of her lips, she turned away. "I'm not sure I want to discuss that at the moment."

Was she upset with him? Gregory wondered. He couldn't tell if the chill he felt was from the atmosphere or the woman seated beside him. In any case, he hadn't had any interactions with her that would result in hostility. As much as he raked his memory, he couldn't seem to think of anything he'd done to draw her ire.

It was probably just his imagination, Gregory thought. He was acting out of character lately, behaving in ways that were contradictory to his logical mind. Practically, it made perfect sense to keep his distance from Liana to avoid being an obstacle in her career decisions. Yet, he found himself seeking her out, ruled more by his heart than his brain.

Maybe he should just let it go, he thought, stand up right now and retreat to the safety of the ballroom. And let the night pass without seeking her attention and potentially saying words he was not meant to say.

But he was a fool if he ever thought he could resist her. He had watched her all evening, his pulse racing each time she smiled and moved with effortless grace. And when she danced, it had taken everything in him to keep from taking her out of Lord Gansey's grasp and declaring to the entire ballroom that she was his.

"I came because I wondered if you might be out here," he said, his voice quieter than usual.

"And if I hadn't been?" She asked, avoiding his eyes as she smoothed her gown.

Gregory drank in the features of her face, letting his eyes trace over the strands of hair that had loosened from her elaborate arrangement and the way her lips parted as though she were catching her breath.

Had she been thinking of him too?

"Then I might have finally let myself forget you."

A sharp exhale left her lips, her fingers curling into the folds of her gown. "That sounds like a lie," she whispered.

It was. It was the biggest lie he had ever told. His lips tugged into something that wasn't quite a smile, and there was no humor in it. "Perhaps," he replied, hesitating as he inhaled deeply and tried to find the right words to say.

But the moment felt too raw, too inevitable. He had spent too many sleepless nights thinking about this woman. Too many hours wondering what might have been. Before he could decide what to say, the words ripped from him in frustration.

"Liana, I can't do this anymore."

She stiffened. "Do what?"

"Pretend," Gregory said hoarsely. His entire body was at war, his mind screaming at him to walk away while his heart wrenched him closer and closer.

"Pretend that I haven't missed you," he continued. "Pretend the distance between us doesn't make my heart ache."

Liana's breath hitched visibly. "Do you truly feel that way? I would never have thought …"

"I don't blame you," Gregory responded. "I'm quite adept at hiding my feelings. It's a side effect of doing business. As I danced with Lady Emma, my true feelings dawned on me."

Liana lifted her chin, a cautious look appearing on her face. "She's a lovely woman."

"She is. A woman with a sensible nature, that's for certain," he admitted, briefly thinking back to how easy it had been to break the news of his disinterest in her.

Gregory saw a flicker of hurt in Liana's eyes. It was so brief that he almost missed it. And yet, he had seen it.

He let out a humorless laugh. "You're waiting for me to say I want her, aren't you?"

Her gaze shifted away. "I wouldn't blame you if you did."

Gregory drew closer. "But I don't."

Liana's eyes widened in surprise.

"She doesn't consume me the way you do," he murmured. "No one else could ever have as much impact on me."

"That isn't very sensible of you," she said softly.

"It isn't, indeed," he said in agreement. His voice was thick with emotion and unsaid words. "If I had any sense at all, I wouldn't be here."

His thumb brushed along the curve of her jaw, all shades of reverent and dangerous.

"And yet," he whispered. "Here I am."

Liana gave a weak smile, a look of disbelief crossing her features. "Do you truly mean what you've just said?"

"Absolutely. I don't want Lady Emma. I want you."

"I'm foolish, Gregory," she whispered as if admitting a terrible sin. "So foolish that I let myself fall in love with you over and over, despite knowing that your pride would stand in the way of your returning my intense feelings."

His eyes darkened. How could she be so painfully unaware?

"You think I don't love you?"

She said nothing, only staring back at him with uncertain eyes.

"Whatever feelings you have for me, know that I feel equal amounts or perhaps even double of it," he began, capturing her in an intense gaze. "As far as decisions go, I'm aware that mine is a terrible one. Because there's no guarantee that you won't cast me aside again."

Pain flickered in her eyes. "Gregory, I ..."

"Tell me," he said, cutting her off. "If we had never met again, would you have sought me out? Or would you have convinced yourself I was better off without you?"

Tears appeared in her eyes. "I didn't let you go because I stopped loving you."

He flinched, overcome by the sheer honesty and care in her voice.

"I let you go because I loved you too much to hold you back," she continued, her voice wavering. "You had the world waiting for you, Gregory, and I ... I would have been selfish to insist that you remain with me."

Gregory exhaled sharply, lifting a hand to caress Liana's cheek gently. "How the tides have turned," he murmured in a tone devoid of humor. "Now I'm forced to make the same decision. I have no choice but to let you go."

Liana gasped loudly, as though she had just stumbled upon a new kind of epiphany. "That was why you stayed away from me," she said slowly, a look of surprise crossing over her features. "Because you assumed that I was going to take up Mr. Barrow's offer."

"I had no way of being certain, but I did come to the conclusion that it was too good an offer to pass up," Gregory admitted.

Liana paused and stared at him, something fierce and determined flickering over her face.

"I am going to perform," she said at last. "But not in New York. Not in a place that takes me away from you."

"You shouldn't have to sacrifice your future—"

"I'm not," she cut in. "The other day, I arranged a deal with Mr. Barrow to begin my career here in England. It will not be as easy as in New York, and I expect to face some backlash. Therefore, I shall begin by performing at private events."

Her words echoed in Gregory's mind until he eventually made sense of it all. She was staying! Something in him broke, then healed, then broke again. His heart sang in excitement, and, urged by the loving look in Liana's eyes, he reached out and cupped her face in both hands.

A slight gasp escaped Liana, but there was an encouraging smile on her face. When their lips met, it had the effect of a thousand volcanoes erupting at the same time. Every wall, every bitter memory, every year of loneliness spent apart melted in that moment.

He kissed her as though she had always belonged to him. As if she were the only thing in the world that mattered. And by every standard possible, she was.

When they finally pulled apart, Gregory found Liana's fingers and interlaced them with his.

"You're mine, Liana," he whispered in a hoarse voice. "Now and always."

She smiled softly, her reddening face visible in the darkness. "And you," she murmured, tracing the outline of his jaw with her other hand, "have always been mine."

And damn it all, nothing else could be more true.

"I'll be honest. I think another heartbreak from you would probably shatter me forever. Logically, this is a risk I shouldn't be taking."

"I won't let you go ever again," Liana said in a voice filled with certainty. "Even if I have to die to keep that promise."

Gregory inhaled sharply, his hand tightening around hers as though he feared she would disappear. Except he knew he'd never let that happen. He would hold on with every breath. She wouldn't turn away from him. Not this time.

Chapter Thirteen

The following day, Liana awoke from the best sleep she'd had in a long while. After her intense night with Gregory, which began as a disaster but ended with her finding love again, she was at peace.

When she ran out of the ballroom as fast as her legs could carry her, she'd been unsure of what the future held. In that moment, all she could think of was the effect of her encounter with Gregory and how much it affected her psyche.

Perhaps it was the way Gregory's hands had felt on her, firm but reverent, as they moved in agonizing synchrony across the dance floor. Or maybe it was the way he had looked at her, his gaze cryptic and unreadable, as though it was full of secrets he could not divulge.

Or maybe it was the undeniable realization that even after all those years, even after the pain and arguments, she was still helplessly and irrevocably in love with him.

Still, none of those assessments had helped. As soon as she sat beneath the giant oak tree in the quiet of the garden, her mind had turned over the events in the ballroom repeatedly. The after-scent of the rain did nothing to cleanse the fire in her blood. The stillness of the night did nothing to silence the echoes of their recent dance and how his touch had branded her through layers of lace.

His presence didn't make things any better at first. Her thought processes were a mess and seeing him only made the confusion worse. She'd been overcome by an urge to blurt out how she felt, and, contrastingly, to say nothing and maintain her dignity.

However, as they talked, she had begun to realize the reason behind his actions and why it was best for her to understand him. Liana smiled, recalling how pleased he'd seemed when she announced that she would be staying in England. She'd never seen a man look so joyous.

Then there was his brief pause as he processed her statement, which was the most attractive thing she had ever had the privilege to witness. And then in the next instant he was kissing her.

It was the most perfect kiss ever, Liana thought dreamily, serving as an appropriate ending to what began as a turbulent night. It was four years of longing, heartbreak, and unspoken love colliding at once.

Still smiling at the memory, Liana arose from her bed and drew the curtains apart. Sunlight streamed into the room, providing more warmth to her already sunny disposition. She hadn't been this excited for a morning at Ravenmoore in ages.

The terrace was awash with the golden light of late afternoon. The air held the thrill of summer, warm yet gentle, with occasional ripples of laughter from the guests. Alexander had sent news that he was inviting a few guests to a game of cards and casual wagers later that afternoon, and Liana knew he would most definitely invite Gregory. This, in turn, meant that she would spend time with him all afternoon.

She lazed around all morning with Dora, recounting events from the past night, both of them giggling in excitement as they talked about it. When afternoon rolled around, Liana welcomed it with a frenzy of preparation. She already had a nice idea of what to wear. A peach sundress that complemented her ivory skin perfectly. Her hair was packed neatly into a bun, and a golden necklace hung delicate from her neck, emphasizing her slender neckline.

Liana had always enjoyed cool afternoons when the sky turned liquid amber, the soft hum of conversation floated through the air, and she could feel the coolness of the surface beneath her fingertips as she traced absent patterns on the table.

However, today there was something even more intoxicating. Gregory was seated beside her. Close enough that when he shifted, the slightest brush of his thigh against hers sent a rush of awareness up her spine. It was utterly ridiculous how much that simple fact delighted her.

Ever the charismatic host, Alexander had arranged an afternoon of whist and witty conversations. Someone was entertaining the group with an account of how his horse had run away for a few weeks before being found in an orchard with nearly all the apples devoured. The orchard belonged to a neighbor, who received the news with great amusement. The story was told with just the right amount of intrigue, and by the end, everyone listening was laughing.

Liana only half-listened to the story, her attention captured by the man seated next to her. The man who had confessed how much he loved her the previous night. Her insides were giddy from positive excitement. She sat with measured poise, her fingers tightly curled around her cards, while her heart thudded wildly against her ribs.

Meanwhile, Gregory appeared completely at ease, shuffling his cards with practiced confidence. It was a considerable change from how he had looked a couple of minutes before, when she appeared on the terrace. A look of awe had appeared on his face, and Liana knew the sundress had accomplished what she hoped it would by taking his breath away.

"You two may as well forfeit the game," Dora announced, breaking Liana away from her thoughts. She was seated on the other side of Gregory, a knowing smirk lingering on her lips. "You're too distracted to play properly."

Liana tilted her head at her. "I'm perfectly capable of playing a game of whist without distraction."

Dora tapped her lips, feigning consideration. "Really? If so, then explain why you just discarded the ace of hearts instead of playing it."

Liana blinked down at her cards. Indeed, there it lay. Utterly wasted.

Gregory, the traitor, chuckled beside her. "So, this is your strategy," he teased gently. "Throwing away perfectly good hands and charming your opponent into submission."

Liana attempted an offended frown, but it was difficult to hide the smile on her face. "Oh, and I suppose you find this amusing?"

His lips twitched. "Deeply."

Dora sighed dramatically. "I fear we must all suffer through the nauseating spectacle of this rekindled romance."

From across the table, Alexander shot a chiding glance in their direction. "Dora, I beg of you, do not harass the guests."

"I would never," Dora replied, eyes twinkling. "Although I do wonder if I should have placed a wager on how long it would take before Gregory inevitably surrendered to Liana's charms."

Gregory exhaled a mock long-suffering sigh, setting down his cards. "If I were a wise man, I would have stayed far away."

Liana's mouth fell open, and as she prepared a retort, he leaned in slightly and added, just for her: "Yet here I am at your mercy, my lady."

His closeness sent a pleasant thrill through her. His voice was low and intimate, a whisper of something dangerous, something unfinished. Even without looking at him, she was certain that he could see how much his words affected her.

Their game continued, though Liana could scarcely concentrate. She was too aware of the way Gregory's gaze lingered on her, the way his fingers curled against his cards as he pondered the next moves to make. She had spent years trying to forget what it felt like to be near him. And now that he was here, solid, warm, and familiar in a way that shattered her resolve, she knew she would never survive another separation.

And judging from how intensely he'd looked at her the previous night, he felt the same.

The love they shared now was perhaps even better than that of the past. They were both older and well-versed in the language of love, which ...

"Lady Liana," A smooth, polite voice called, interrupting the moment.

Liana turned to see Lord Gansey, the same gentleman who had asked her to dance during the ball. She sighed inwardly, knowing that she would have to kindly let him down. There were several other ladies at the manor who would appreciate his disposition and titles better than she did.

She felt Gregory's gaze on her as she addressed Lord Gansey. "Yes?"

"I hope I'm not interrupting," Lord Gansey said. "But I was hoping for a moment of your time."

Liana hesitated. As much as she longed to honor his request and hear what he wanted to say, she was far too comfortable dwelling in Gregory's presence to disrupt the lovely moment.

To her absolute horror, Dora spoke for her. "I believe Lady Liana has something presently occupying her time," she said sweetly. "But if you insist, I suppose we can spare her."

Liana shot her a look of betrayal, but Dora only winked in response. Her sister had the tendency to put her in difficult spots, believing that it would help her become more firm and outspoken. That had served her greatly on some occasions, and in others, like this one, it brought about some anxiety.

Gregory said nothing, but the way his body stiffened, and his eyes lingered on her expressed his thoughts. No doubt, he was already aware of Lord Gansey's interest in her.

She was going to let him down kindly, Liana decided as she rose from her seat and allowed Lord Gansey to lead the way. Once they were in the cool embrace of the hallway, she sighed softly, gathering her composure.

"Lady Liana," Lord Gansey began hesitantly. "Forgive me for my directness, but I have grown ... quite fond of your company."

"That is rather kind of you to say, my lord," Liana replied, choosing her words carefully.

"My heart is earnest, and I'd like to confirm that you're not indifferent to me," he said, his tone hopeful.

"I do enjoy your company," Liana admitted, because it was true. Lord Gansey was kind, thoughtful, and deserving of love. But not her love. "However, what you're insinuating is impossible."

His face fell when she finished her statement. "Your heart belongs to another," he said softly.

Liana nodded. "Yes. I am absolutely certain of it."

Lord Gansey nodded slowly before bowing his head in resignation. "Then I shall not make a fool of myself by pressing further. I truly hope that you'll find happiness with the man you've chosen."

Liana reached forward, giving his hand a gentle squeeze. "And I hope the same for you."

* * *

Meanwhile, Gregory watched as Liana and her persistent admirer walked away. As he did so, he registered the familiar pang of jealousy. Before he could fully dwell on it, he felt a tap on his shoulder.

"Well, Mr. Holt," she said in a drawl. "You look positively murderous."

Gregory took a measured sip of his drink. "I'm not murderous."

"Are you sure? Because you look as if you'd like to toss Lord Gansey into the sea."

He exhaled slowly. "He's unworthy of her."

Dora's smile widened. "If you want to convince me that you don't care, you're doing a terrible job of it."

Gregory set his glass down with precision. "You are insufferable."

Dora sighed satisfactorily. "I know." A silent moment passed before she turned serious. "You do realize you're not the only one who is blindly in love, don't you?"

"What are you talking about?" he asked, providing his full attention.

Dora's expression softened. "Liana."

The sound of her name caused happy bells to ring in his head.

"She adores you, Gregory," Dora said. "She always has. She wrote you letters, in fact."

Gregory listened fully, intrigued by the statements being uttered.

"Dozens of them," Dora continued. "She never sent them, but I've seen them. She was never indifferent to you, no matter how it may have seemed."

That much was true and believable. He'd been too stubborn to accept that in the past, but now he knew better.

Dora leaned in, as if to emphasize her next statements. "Liana is sacrificial by nature. She thought that letting you go was what you needed and suffered for it. You weren't the only one with a broken heart. In conclusion, just as much as you're smitten by Liana, she's equally smitten with you. There's nothing to worry about."

Having confirmation that Liana pined for him over the years that he had been away only served to make Gregory feel better. He vowed to fill their coming years with much joy; the four years they had spent apart didn't matter. It was also relieving to know that Liana's decision to let him go had not been made with ease.

When Liana returned, she took the seat beside him once again. There was a relieved look on her face, a sign that the conversation with Lord Gansey had gone well.

Dora turned to Liana with a knowing smile. "Judging by Lord Gansey's downcast expression, I presume you let him down gently?"

Liana nodded. "I didn't want him to keep holding on to false hopes."

Gregory's grip on his wine glass loosened. Clearly, he'd been more worried and jealous than he realized. She had let Lord Gansey down, which further confirmed what Dora was saying.

Liana wasn't the sort of woman to string two suitors along or act in ways that could hurt him on purpose. The man she had tried to let go of was still the only one she wanted.

Shortly afterwards, they excused themselves from the table and went for a walk in the garden.

"I had a talk with Dora while you were with Lord Gansey," Gregory said.

"Oh no!" Liana exclaimed. "What did she say this time?"

Gregory laughed at the rawness of Liana's reaction. Not that it was without reason—Dora could be quite garrulous at times. "If I recall correctly, you wrote letters but never sent them to me?"

"That's true," Liana replied. "I shared that news with you once before."

"You're right," Gregory said, recalling how she'd previously tried to convince him that she still cared for him, but he'd been too stubborn then to listen. "Why did you choose to suffer, Liana? Nothing was stopping you from moving on and choosing to forget me."

"At the time, I thought it was for the best," she responded. "Now I know better. I really do."

They had come to a part of the garden that was out of view from the manor. Four years ago, they had walked to this part of the estate when they sought privacy.

Gregory turned to face her earnestly, cupping her face in his hands. "Liana, my love, you'll never have to suffer in silence again."

Liana giggled, looking even more beautiful as she blushed. "I believe every bit of that statement."

Recalling Dora's words about how Liana was equally smitten with him, something dawned on him.

"You!" He exclaimed.

She blinked, her eyebrows furrowing in confusion. "Me?"

"It was you," he murmured, his thoughts coming together. "You're the one who sent those drinks after a long day's work with your brother. You made them with my favorite fruits, being the most likely one to know that information."

A slow, guilty smile played on her lips. "I thought you'd never notice."

"I do now," Gregory replied, a raw and vulnerable feeling occupying his heart. He linked their fingers together and squeezed gently. "And I promise to repay that favor a thousand times over."

Chapter Fourteen

Liana's eyes fluttered open to the gentle murmur of birdsong and the soft rustling of leaves overhead. A cool breeze stirred the air, mingling with the warmth of the afternoon sun on her cheeks. Lodged deeply within her was the joyful sensation that came along with being around the person one loved.

She made a little sound of contentment and sat upright on the wooden bench beneath the great elm, her gaze drifting toward the lake glistening a short distance away. The faint rustling of leaves and the familiar hum of water lapping against the lakeshore filled the air.

Liana's stomach grumbled, and a rustle drew her attention to the figure arranging a small, well-packed basket on a blanket not far off. Gregory, with his sleeves lightly rolled and hair slightly tousled from the breeze, turned toward her with a smile that reached his eyes.

"You were quite determined to rest," he said, rising to his feet. "I thought it best not to wake you."

Liana blushed faintly. "I only meant to close my eyes for a moment."

"It ended up being closer to twenty," he replied, checking the timepiece in his coat pocket. "But you looked peaceful. I thought it better to let you dream."

He gestured to the picnic beside him. "I took the liberty of asking the housekeeper for a light repast. I remembered you used to love the bread from Mrs. Fenton's oven."

The scent of warm bread and jam reached her, and her stomach let out a gentle protest of hunger. She rose and approached the spread—nothing extravagant, just sliced fruit, bread, and sweetmeats laid out with quiet thoughtfulness.

"You remembered," she said softly.

"Of course," Gregory replied. "It's good to be back here with you."

They were back at their meeting spot at the lake, where they used to converse and have lunch together four years ago. In the years when they were apart, Liana had come down here to reminisce about their time spent together. It had seemed then that things would never be the same. Thankfully, the tides of fate had turned, bringing her and Gregory back to their happy place.

The lake was only a short walk from Ravenmoore's gardens. Though no chaperone stood nearby, the proximity to the house made it acceptable—especially given their long acquaintance and the growing understanding between them.

She took a seat across from him on the blanket, careful to keep a modest distance. "It feels like nothing has changed."

"Everything has," he said, eyes on her. "But I find I like the changes."

Liana doubted she would ever get used to the look of adoration on Gregory's face each time he looked at her. It reminded her of the past, when he doted on her and never hesitated to express his feelings. Theirs had been a younger version of love. Now they were older, and their love had grown deeper, blossoming into peak maturity. She would never exchange it for anything else.

"Thank you for this," Liana said, appreciative of his kind efforts.

Gregory waved a hand in dismissal. "A man should always find ways to impress his future wife."

A soft, easy smile was playing on his lips. It was unlike the dismissive glances she'd received on certain occasions while growing up, or the restrained ones he reserved for strangers and colleagues in public. This was different. It was open, unburdened.

"I'll do this for you a thousand times over," he added.

Liana's heart fluttered in response to his words. They were technically in the courtship stage, but it would only be a matter of time before Gregory proposed. And soon after that, she'd be living a life she had imagined a thousand times over. Waking up every day as Gregory Holt's wife.

"You're making it very difficult not to love you," she said, smiling shyly.

His voice softened. "Then don't try."

They ate in comfortable silence for a while, sharing little remarks and laughter. When he passed her a slice of apple, their fingers brushed, and the warmth that shot through her was far stronger than any summer sun.

"I barely slept last night," she divulged. "That must be the reason why I was so tired today."

Gregory stared at her in concern. "Why not?"

"I kept thinking about the future," she explained. "About us and what it would be with you. To wake up beside you every morning. To know that I'd never have to be without you ever again."

His expression softened. "You won't have to think for long. I intend for us to be married once all proper arrangements have been made."

She smiled shyly. "Speaking of which, I have already begun thinking about the wedding."

He straightened his spine, a flicker of curiosity and amusement in his gaze. "And?"

Liana blushed. "I'd like a small wedding."

Gregory laughed. "For a Foxworth, that's practically unheard of."

"What do you mean by that?" Liana asked with a smile, already knowing what he was referring to.

A line of her ancestors was renowned for being lavish, and in the past, they had often held weekly events that drew in great crowds. One of the most legendary was a wedding the queen was rumored to have attended personally, and it was said that the event had cost over a hundred thousand pounds.

"Your ancestors would be flabbergasted if they heard you say this," he teased.

"The lavish Foxworths were only a small line in a long list of others who were often reasonable and kind. My great-grandfather used to organize feasts in certain areas in London in order to feed the poor. I like to imagine that my calm personality was inherited from him."

"If that's the case, then I owe him quite a lot," Gregory said, the sight of his smile resulting in a happy thrill through her heart. "Now let's return to our earlier subject. I desire to provide a wedding that's worthy of you. It need not be lavish, but I suspect that it will be by the time we're done with the calculations. Wait till we're knee-deep in floral arrangements and your sister begins importing flowers from France. Or your brother begins inviting acquaintances from all over the world to the wedding."

"I understand why you would say that," she replied. "But I'd like to insist on the financial costs being low or moderate. I'll be sure to communicate this to everyone else as well. It's only a wedding, after all."

"You truly intend to stand by this," Gregory said, realization dawning in his eyes. He drew closer and bopped her nose lovingly. "I have never seen you look so determined. Very well, you shall have your preference. You're an intriguing woman, Liana. There's so much that goes on in your head, and it's always a delight hearing you speak."

"Thank you," she said, blushing furiously. "I hope this doesn't affect your image of what our wedding would be like."

"Not at all. It is rare for women of your class to have modest weddings, but there are always exceptions to the rule. Still, I expect that our wedding will cause a minor stir in society. Your brother is an earl, after all, and the guest list, if left uncontrolled, could populate a small kingdom."

"Don't leave out the fact that I'm marrying a wealthy businessman," she added. "This is also a largely beneficial arrangement to me."

With his line of successful businesses, Gregory was undoubtedly a very wealthy man. And if his new venture went as expected, his assets would only continue to grow. She was certain that most people would discuss only the benefit of Gregory's marrying into the distinguished Foxworth family, which was why she thought it necessary to highlight that it was an equal union.

Moreover, even if he were poor, she would still marry him, and it was clear that he'd do the same in the reverse situation.

"Tell me what your ideal wedding looks like," Gregory murmured.

"I want something intimate, with just family and friends in attendance. I'd like plenty of flowers everywhere, making the venue incredibly welcoming."

She had always loved flowers, after all, and it would not be her wedding without swarms of them everywhere.

Gregory reached for her hand, his thumb grazing softly over her knuckles. "I'll make whatever you want happen, no matter the difficulty. I promise you that."

"Thank you," she murmured, overcome by affection and gratitude.

When her eyes returned to Gregory, she noticed that he was studying her, his gaze lingering in that unique way that made her feel entirely seen.

Liana's cheeks warmed. "Why are you staring at me like that?"

Gregory tilted his head slightly, a look of increased awareness dawning in his eyes. "I finally understand why I'm so drawn to you."

She blinked in puzzlement. "Are you referring to the biological aspect? I've been told that the mixture of hormones makes a person more attractive to someone else, and that's how love is born."

He laughed and shook his head. "No." Tugging her hand, he pulled her closer. "It is because you have a heart that humbles mine."

He reached out—and after the briefest hesitation—brushed a stray curl from her cheek, his gloved fingers gentle and reverent. Her breath caught at the contact, and she leaned ever so lightly into his touch.

"I've done many things in the name of ambition. I've made ruthless decisions, negotiated with cutthroats, and taken risks most men wouldn't dare. It's made me successful. But you ..."

He exhaled, caressing the side of her face gently. She leaned into his touch, having realized that it was a deeply soothing gesture.

"Being with you settles my soul," he said finally.

She could identify the sincerity in his voice and was touched by it.

"I think you may have overestimated my importance, Gregory Holt."

"On the contrary," he murmured. "Your importance requires more attention and praise."

Liana laughed teasingly. "You always sound so certain about everything. Have you considered that you might be wrong?"

"Not in this instance," Gregory responded simply. "And I intend to spend the rest of my life proving it."

They spent the rest of the afternoon eating lunch and listening to the lake water as it rippled quietly. Once they finished their meals, Gregory returned the empty plates to a basket they'd brought along, his movements unhurried and content. Liana lay on her back and stared at the cozy afternoon sky, feeling utterly at peace.

"This is perfect," she murmured.

Gregory smirked. "I'm excellent company, aren't I?"

Laughing quietly, she fetched a grape and threw it in his direction. He caught it midair and popped it into his mouth with an answering grin.

Liana rolled onto her side, propping herself up on an elbow with a thoughtful look on her face. "You are, truly. You make me feel very valued," she tucked a strand of hair behind her ear before continuing. "You see ... I've spent so much of my life placing everyone else ahead of myself."

Gregory nodded in agreement. "I know that for certain."

She sat up and glanced at the manor in the distance. "It's why I like being at Ravenmoore. Alexander needs help managing events, and I like assisting where I can. I like knowing that I can make things easier for people."

Gregory reached over, taking her hand in his. "That's admirable, Liana. But you deserve happiness too."

She looked away, momentarily struck by the unshakable certainty in his voice.

He cupped her chin, gently tilting her face back toward him. "You're allowed to prioritize yourself, Liana. You're as important as everyone else."

She swallowed, lost in his emerald gaze. "I ... I wouldn't even know how."

"Then I'll teach you," he murmured.

"You will?" She asked, searching his face.

"Of course," he responded. "I'm going to prove that you deserve everything good and more. Starting today, I want you to do things that make you happy."

Liana hesitated briefly before replying slowly, "I think ... I think I already did."

"Oh?" He questioned with a raised eyebrow. "Do tell."

"Chasing after you was the first thing I had ever done for myself," she said with a proud smile. "Not giving up on you, even when you rejected me. That was my first act of choosing myself."

Gregory's gaze softened, and his face was filled with something deep and raw. He brushed a slow kiss against her knuckles. "Then I shall make it worth the choosing. Every day."

She smiled softly. "Thank you."

He sat next to her and took her hand in his. His grip tightened slightly as his thumb brushed over her pulse.

"Liana," he muttered, his voice dropping in a low, serious tone. "You were right, after all."

Her eyebrows furrowed. "About what?"

Gregory inhaled deeply. "About choosing yourself. About us." He reached over and cupped her face in his gentle but firm grasp. "Four years ago, I should have fought harder for you. I should have chased after you the same way you did for me."

Liana swallowed thickly, her heart aching due to the weight of his words. "You're here now," she whispered.

His jaw clenched as his thumb traced a slow, reverent path along her cheekbone. "I refuse to waste another moment," he murmured. "I won't let you go again. Not unless … you want me to."

Liana exhaled deeply, leaning over to press her forehead against his. "What makes you think I'll ever want to? That will never occur. In addition, I don't think you really did let me go," she admitted. "I suspect that I was always present in your mind in some capacity, only you didn't wish to acknowledge it."

Gregory stilled. Then, slowly and deliberately, he squeezed her hand. It was a small gesture, but it signaled more. A sense of togetherness. New beginnings.

As they sat together, Liana realized something.

She would never be alone again.

She was home.

Chapter Fifteen

The next few days were nothing short of delightful for Liana. Her experiences with Gregory had left her floating in the clouds, all smiles and no objections. He was just as he was four years ago, except even better. Now he was more attentive, relaxed, and mature. She felt as though she were occupying a long-lost dream, except this time it was real.

Liana smiled to herself as she strolled through the garden. This was the first day in a long while that she would be by herself. Gregory and some of the other men had gone out for a hunt, leaving those uninterested and the women at the estate. These were often delightful moments because it meant those present at the manor could have fewer people around and enjoy some serenity before the men returned. But for Liana, it was a gruesome moment. She would have to enjoy her own company all morning without Gregory by her side. That was an act she'd grown unaccustomed to from the events of the past days.

She caressed a flower gently, blushing at the memories of her and Gregory on the carefully cut grass. She sat on a stone bench in the garden, the warm afternoon air tickling the edges of her dress. The world felt different today. Or perhaps she felt different. She let her eyes drift to the roses in full bloom, their petals opening eagerly to the sun, their fragrance thick and sweet in the air.

A few days ago, she might have passed them without a second thought. But today, everything felt sharper, more vivid, as if she had been wandering through life in muted colors and now, all of a sudden, she could see. She traced her fingers along the stone beneath her, inhaling deeply.

Gregory.

Her thoughts flew to him with decisive eagerness. Her mind grew with memories of them seated together on the bench as the ball went on. Even now, days later, her skin still tingled with the memory of his hands and the way his lips had felt against hers, warm and devastatingly familiar.

Her smile grew even wider as she recalled their time at the lake and how they'd jumped into the water together. It was such a foolish, impulsive thing to do, something she never would have considered before. She had spent years thinking practically and always ensuring that her choices were measured and selfless.

And yet, in that moment, she had let go. Due to Gregory's prompting, she'd done something new, and it felt exhilarating. She could fall because she knew he would catch her. She had laughed. She had lived. And he had kissed her.

Liana closed her eyes, feeling a rush of joy as familiar feelings raced through her. Their time together at the lake had been everything. It wasn't just about the pleasure of his company, although that had been enough to undo her entirely. It was about the pure emotions evoked by his affection.

Gregory had spoken to her and held her with immense care, as though he had finally yielded to a powerful inclination. As if he'd recognized a profound desire, he had long resisted.

Years had passed since they were two love-struck young people who were deeply in love. Yet, as she spent time in his company, she felt as though the years had not intervened

In the time they had been apart, Liana had feared that perhaps things had changed too much. That too many things had been left unsaid, and the only foreseeable future was one in which they were strangers instead of lovers.

But she had been wrong.

Everything was the same and arguably even better. The fluttering of her heart, the lingering pull of his gaze, the tenderness in his voice. It was entirely perfect.

Her fingers curled into the fabric of her gown as she exhaled slowly. But what now? They had discussed the terms of their wedding, so it wouldn't be too presumptuous to assume that they would be married soon.

Although she wasn't in the habit of dwelling on terrible thoughts, she tried to imagine what life would look like without Gregory in it. If by some unfortunate twist of fate, he went off in another direction without asking her to come along. Or if he woke up the very next day, regretting their reunion and breaking things off.

A sharp pang lanced through her chest at the idea. She'd given him up before, after convincing herself that it was the right thing to do. She'd told herself that his success, his future, his ambitions, were more important than her own heartache.

Could she survive going through that again?

A gust of wind carried the scent of flowers toward her, but it did little to soothe the tightness in her chest. She wished she could silence the doubtful thoughts creeping into her mind. She wished Gregory were here to banish them with a single touch, a single whispered reassurance.

Next, she thought of their morning rides and how his laughter had become a sound she cherished. She'd memorized the way the sunlight hit his face whenever he turned toward her.

She recalled the other night in the garden and the conversation that passed between them. The tension had been fraught and rigid until they both made the decision to have a clear conversation. Through this, they were able to work out the grudges and misunderstandings that had previously plagued them. And as they began to understand each other, it felt like the world had rearranged itself to make sense again.

A realization struck her suddenly, settling deep into her bones. She had loved him before, but this was different. This was a love forged through pain, time, and absence. It had endured and would continue to, even when obstacles emerged and attempted to break it.

A shadow fell over her, pulling her from her thoughts.

"Lady Liana?" the direct voice prompted.

Liana raised her head to see Lady Emma standing a few feet away, her gloved hands clasped together in a polite but speculative stance.

"Lady Emma," Liana greeted, smoothing her dress as she arose.

"Call me Emma," the other woman replied with a friendly smile. "I believe it's high time we dropped these tiresome formalities, don't you think? It only stands in the way of us getting to know each other better."

Liana nodded. "In that case, you can call me Liana."

Emma tilted her head slightly, studying her. "Forgive me if I'm intruding, but you looked ... rather lost in thought."

Liana let out a small laugh. "I suppose I was."

Emma nodded in understanding, stepping closer. "Would you care for a walk? I find movement often helps untangle one's thoughts."

Liana hesitated. Did she truly wish to spend time with the woman Gregory had once entertained as a potential match? It certainly seemed odd. Then, realizing how ridiculous she was being, she smiled. "That would be lovely."

They strolled along the garden path, the soft crunch of gravel beneath their feet. The silence was deafening as Liana wondered what Emma could be thinking about. Thankfully, Emma broke the silence before too long.

"You and Mr. Holt seem …quite comfortable in each other's company," she said.

Liana's heart jumped, but she kept her face even. She was aware that everyone at the estate had been talking about them lately. Even Dora could barely keep a straight face around her these days. How could they not? Gregory had made his affections for her public. He was always present to escort her to dinner, was the first gentleman to ask her to dance during balls, and usually sat beside her during social events. The sudden realization that they were being watched through all that made her feel embarrassed.

"We have known each other for quite some time," Liana replied.

"Yes, I gathered as much," Emma said. She hesitated, then added, "I must admit, it is rare to see … such intensity between two people."

Liana turned to her, but Emma was gazing ahead with a thoughtful expression.

"I wonder," Emma continued, smiling lightly. "What it must feel like to love someone so deeply that the very air between you feels charged."

Liana swallowed. Without a doubt, the relationship between her and Gregory had sparked a kind of reaction among observers. She recalled a brief conversation during which Dora had playfully shared that some of the women present at the manor now woke up early to watch her horse rides with Gregory. She had thought of it as a joke, but now she suspected there was more to it. For the women, watching them provided a lovely sensation, a sight they could swoon over. On the other hand, the men probably felt encouraged to show affection in the way Gregory did.

Everyone desired to make the passion between themselves and their partners burn actively. Perhaps that was a positive outcome.

"You speak as though you've never experienced such a thing yourself," Liana stated, finally finding her voice.

Emma let out a soft, wry laugh. "I have not."

Liana furrowed her brow. "But surely you've had suitors?"

"Oh, plenty," Emma responded with another charming smile. She was a beautiful woman, and only the blind would be compelled to argue otherwise. "Men who admired my intellect. Men who found me agreeable. Others who saw me as a suitable match."

She paused to gaze ahead again before continuing, "But never a man who looked at me the way Mr. Holt looks at you."

Liana's breath caught in her throat. Emma reminded her of Gregory in some ways. She was blunt and straightforward, but also skilled at skirting through words without coming off as impolite. If she were a man, Liana had no doubt that Emma would be a learned graduate from Eton or some other prestigious university.

Emma turned to her then, offering a small, knowing smile. "You are very fortunate, Liana."

Liana exhaled shakily, her fingers brushing over the lace of her sleeve. "It has not always felt like good fortune."

Emma nodded. "Love often doesn't. It is not always kind and simple."

They walked in silence for a while as the sun dipped lower in the sky.

Then quietly, Emma said, "I have always considered myself a practical woman, you know. I have never been one to indulge in overly romantic notions."

Liana tilted her head, flattered and honored that the other woman was willing to share so much of herself. "And yet?"

Emma released a slow breath, her gaze drifting to the flowers lining the path. "And yet, watching you and Mr. Holt has made me wonder …" she hesitated. "Perhaps there is something to be said for abandoning practicality, just once, in favor of passion."

Liana smiled softly. "It's a rather uncertain path."

"Yes. But I suspect it is worth it."

Liana thought of Gregory's eyes and the way he looked at her, of the sound of her name on his lips, and how he seemed to be immensely strong and yet fragile in an understandable parallel.

She thought about how hard her life had been four years ago. How she cried all day, her heart aching due to his absence. Then there were the events from past weeks, part of which she spent watching Gregory as he spent time with Lady Emma.

Her mind turned to the night of the ball and how things had improved greatly afterwards. Now it was like they had never been apart. More than ever, she believed that this time they would get it right.

"I think loving someone selflessly does require letting go of practicality to a certain extent. It is indeed an indescribable feeling, and I do hope you get to experience it soon enough," Liana said.

"Thank you," the other woman replied with a grateful look. "Kindly excuse me, Liana. I must head back inside. It was a delight having this conversation with you."

"The pleasure's mine. I've always admired how graceful you seem to be, no matter the situation, and I have enjoyed speaking to you as well."

With a friendly wave, Emma departed from the garden. Liana returned to the stone bench, her mind racing from the conversation she'd just had. Emma was certainly a brilliant woman, one who would make a fine wife for the right gentleman.

She wasn't a social individual and thus had little knowledge of what type of gentleman might be a good fit for Emma. Otherwise, she might have conspired with Dora to match Emma with a gentleman from Alex's extensive social circle.

On the other hand, Emma likely already had a good number of individuals to pick from. Except none of them seemed like people she could fall in love with. It was a truly perplexing situation.

Liana's lips curved upwards as Emma's words echoed in her mind. *But never a man who looked at me the way Mr. Holt looks at you.*

She pressed a hand to her chest, her heartbeat steadying. That was something even Emma had noticed. The way Gregory looked at her, as though she were something sacred.

For the first time in years, she had everything she wanted. Gregory's love and devotion, the promise that he would never leave her again, and now an occupation to look forward to. In due time, she would begin working with Lord Harper to perform in events that he arranged for her. And if that went well, there would be more memorable performances to come.

This time, she would savor every minute. The life she now lived was one her former self would have looked upon with great envy. She felt like the luckiest woman in the world.

She returned to the manor in high spirits. As she walked along the grand hallways once occupied by her blue-blooded ancestors, her thoughts momentarily drifted to Lady Emma once more. The woman had been practical all her life, but Liana had a feeling that would change soon. It felt nice to have witnessed the dignified, self-possessed Emma, but Liana looked forward to experiencing a more naturally open and casual version of the woman.

Liana entered the drawing room and found Dora seated at the window. Her sister was unnaturally quiet, only mumbling a brief greeting to acknowledge Liana's presence.

"What is it? Why do you look so morose?"

Dora blinked. "In what way?"

"You're always full of energy, even in moments when you've exhausted yourself physically. Did you go horse riding this morning? Is that why you look so spent?"

"I'm *excellent* at horse riding; therefore, such activities do not leave me feeling tired," Dora replied in an indignant tone.

"I know. I was hoping to get a reaction from you by making that statement, and it seems I have achieved it to some extent."

Dora sniffled. "Clearly, the copious amount of time spent in Mr. Holt's company is rubbing off on you. You're more garrulous than usual."

"And you, my dear sister, aren't being forthcoming, which is very unusual. Shall I fetch Alex?"

"No!" Dora objected, reaching out to take Liana's hands. "I fear calling our brother would only complicate matters further."

"In that case, would you please tell me what's going on?" Liana asked softly, her face full of worry. Her sister was all mischief and sharp wit, always poised with a teasing remark or unbridled laughter during hilarious situations. Other than times when she was painting, Dora never allowed silence to settle around her in the way she now did.

"There's no major matter to bother about, so leave your worries at the door," Dora reassured. "I've however come upon something that has left me rather contemplative."

Liana let out a sigh of relief, having been made better by the reassurance that there was no great trouble.

"Do you remember the mysterious gentleman I spoke about?" Dora asked. "One of Alex's guests who has persistently remained out of sight?"

"Why, yes," Liana replied. "As I recall, you were rather insistent on discovering his identity."

"Sometimes I wonder if my stubborn tendencies are a blessing or a curse," her sister replied with a sigh. "In any case, due to my persistence, I managed to discover the mysterious gentleman's identity."

Liana's eyes widened. "Truly? Is that why you were so lost in thought?"

"Indeed, it is."

"Who is it then? You can't just announce that without further elaboration."

"And here's where the twist lies," Dora began. "I have decided not to divulge his identity."

"That's quite unlike you," Liana said. "You've never been the sort to shy away from revealing such information, especially for the sake of gossip."

Dora smiled. "I still am that sort of person. Do not underestimate my penchant for gossip."

"This man must have some kind of hold on you," Liana joked. "He caused you to change your mind about revealing his identity, which is something I couldn't get you to do when we played hiding games as children."

A moment passed before Dora responded. "He didn't try to convince me at all," Her voice held a tone of wonder, as though she were learning something new about herself.

"Not even with a little gift?"

Dora shook her head to say no. "On the contrary, I'm refraining from sharing his identity because it's the right thing to do."

Liana studied her sister as the air whooshed gently around them. Who was this gentleman, and what had he done to make her sister feel so strongly about protecting him?

Chapter Sixteen

For Gregory, the past few weeks at the manor had been filled with conflicting emotions. He'd found out the reason why Liana rebuffed him four years ago, and although it was a selfless reason that helped him achieve greatness, he couldn't help but mourn the time lost during that period. However, there were good things to come. His breakthrough with Alex a few days back was bound to guarantee his complete freedom from his uncle, further increasing his ability to grow independently.

In addition, he and Liana were on good terms again, their relationship blossoming like cherry blossoms at the start of spring. Fragile, delicate, but promising and remarkably beautiful.

As he sat in Radnor's study and the sunlight filtered through the window, Gregory decided life couldn't be any more perfect. He and Alex had sat down together since dawn to finalize the business plans. They had drafted a contract, reviewed it, and it was now time to append their signatures.

This was the start of a new journey to embark on, yet in his heart, it was even more. It was also the beginning of a new bond between him and Radnor, one that transcended their business partnership and lasting friendship. Considering the turn of events with Liana, they would make an official arrangement soon. That meant Alex might soon become his brother-in-law.

He wondered for a second how their connection would evolve. Alex had never interfered in his relationship with Liana, choosing to trust that his close friend and sister were able to manage their own affairs.

When she ended their engagement four years ago, Alex had only offered his commiserations without further deliberation. At first, Gregory had thought that he was upset with him for the manner of their parting, but as time passed, he realized that Alex cared for both his sister and his friend deeply and preferred to let them make their own decisions. It was rather admirable, but it left Gregory worried about what Alex would think of his and Liana's renewed relationship. Would he be relieved that they had resolved matters? Or would he finally share his true opinion on what he thought of their relationship?

With a practiced hand, Alex completed the last of his signatures. The ink on the paper had barely dried when Alex pushed it across the table and leaned back in his chair with a look of mild triumph. The fire in the hearth cracked gently between them, casting long shadows on the richly paneled walls of the study.

"Your turn, my dear friend," he encouraged, the triumphant look still lingering on his face.

Gregory moved his quill fluidly across the paper, flexed his hand, and eyed the signed pages in front of him. "There it is, then," he said. "Done."

In the Foxworth manor, he and Alex had made a plan for a more secure financial future. Similarly, he and Liana had planned for their future. The walls of Radnor's study had been the setting for significant moments in his life so far, he mused, glancing around the finely decorated room. His eyes raked over its rich ebony walls and the array of neatly arranged books appreciatively.

Alex rose to his feet and clapped triumphantly. Gregory had never seen a man who appreciated business dealings as much as the earl.

"With any luck, the manufacturing company will grow bigger than we planned," he said, walking to a corner table with a bottle of brandy and two glasses placed upon it. He turned to Gregory with a grin as he poured out two glasses of brandy and handed one over.

"To lucrative ventures and more achievements."

Gregory took the glass, saying nothing for a moment. He simply returned the smile and raised his glass in salute before drinking the brandy. His thoughts had wandered again, going beyond the matter of business, which was now a resolved issue.

Noticing his taciturn state, Alex returned to sit on the opposite side of Gregory before speaking.

"You've been unusually distracted for a man about to double his holdings, Holt," he noted, swirling his drink in his hands as he eyed Gregory in concern.

Gregory offered a faint smile. "Money's not everything."

"Ha," Alex said dryly, arching a brow with an amused expression on his face. "So, is it love then?"

Gregory glanced into the amber liquid swirling in his glass. "Correct. It's about Liana."

Radnor's expression softened. "You still care for her."

"I never stopped," Gregory admitted. "I was angry. Hurt. I thought I had moved on. But the moment I saw her again, it was as if no time had passed. And now that we're together again, I hope to never let her go."

"She's a good soul, my sister," Alex commented. "I don't doubt that you two would make a wonderful match. Your steely determination in combination with her soft demeanor. She's always loved you. I know you feel the same way, too, but as Liana's brother, I am compelled by duty to say this ... don't make her regret it."

Gregory nodded with a serious expression. "I won't."

A sudden knock on the study door interrupted their conversation. Radnor's staff were rarely in the habit of bothering him when he was in the study, unless there was an emergency.

"Come in."

At the earl's request, a footman entered the study, accompanied by two unfamiliar men in uniform. Both men had stern looks on their faces, and their coats bore the insignia of the London constabulary.

Gregory and the earl exchanged brief, worried looks.

"Good day, gentlemen," Alex greeted calmly, his voice suffused with every bit of authority. "What brings you to Ravenmoore Estate?"

The men removed their hats in sync as they offered their greetings to the earl. "We're looking for Mr. Gregory Holt," one of the constables replied. He was tall and lean, with a plain face that seemed twisted in a perpetual grimace.

Gregory schooled his face to remove any traces of surprise. "Why?"

"To my knowledge, there isn't any reason to have constables at a summer retreat," Alex added in a chiding tone. "What is the matter?"

"I'm afraid this matter concerns Ravenmoore Estate and its occupants, my lord," the other constable said, pinching his ear in what seemed to be a habitual move as he spoke. "You'll want to hear this."

"Well, spit it out, will you?" The earl replied impatiently. "Whatever reason you have to interrupt me in my study must be quite important indeed."

"We received a concerning tip regarding Mr. Holt," the grimacing constable responded. "According to the tip, he intends to murder Lady Emma, and he arrived at Ravenmoore Estate for this purpose."

"We've traveled down from London to follow this tip and detain Mr. Holt while we conduct an investigation," the second constable added.

"This is new to me," Gregory stated in clear shock. "I'm many things, but not a murderer, and I've never had bad intentions for Lady Emma."

"Well, sir, it is our duty to investigate and determine who is truly innocent," the first constable said.

"What a ridiculous accusation," Alex said coldly. Turning to a footman, he barked a command. "Where's Lady Emma? Fetch her right away so she can refute these baseless statements."

The footman rushed out in urgency, and Alex turned to the constables with a diplomatic smile. "I'm certain this is all a misunderstanding. Lady Emma has been present at Ravenmoore Estate for weeks now, and I can confirm that she's perfectly well."

"Lord Radnor, the anonymous tip didn't say Mr. Holt had committed the crime. We were told that he plans to; therefore, we're here to ensure that doesn't happen," the ear-pinching constable said.

"Either way, Gregory isn't guilty of what you speak of," Alex said sternly.

The footman soon returned, accompanied by a young woman whom Gregory recognized as Lady Emma's maid. He couldn't say anything, too shocked by the event that had just transpired. He could only watch as matters unfolded

"Where is Lady Emma, and why are you here instead?" Alex demanded of the maid.

"My lord, we wanted to tell you but waited because you were busy with Mr. Holt," the woman said, trembling due to a mix of awe and fear. "Lady Emma's tea was laced with something terrible. She has been unconscious ever since, and her breathing is weak."

"When did this occur?" Gregory asked.

"Only this morning, sir. We do not know when she took the tea, but it appears to be poisoned."

"Well, it appears we're too late," one of the constables said to the other, before advancing toward Gregory. "Mr. Holt, I'm afraid we have to take you with us."

"Stop," Alex commanded. "Nobody leaves. This is my estate, and I will ensure that everyone is safe. Please give us time to investigate what happened here. Lady Emma and Mr. Holt are both distinguished guests of mine, and it is my duty to get to the bottom of this. That would also aid in securing the trust of future guests at Ravenmoore."

The two constables exchanged another glance before nodding calmly. It was clear that their respect for the earl overruled the urge to make impulsive judgments.

"We shall carry out investigations at once," the first constable replied. "In the meantime, no one leaves the estate, Mr. Holt included."

"I can assure you of that," Alex responded.

Gregory remained in his seat, rigid and motionless. He was simply too shocked to consider acting in a different way. His thoughts flitted about in different directions, but one remained consistent. Who could have harmed Lady Emma, and what could their motive be? His fists instinctively clenched at his sides as his mind wandered.

"Fetch Lady Liana immediately," he heard Lord Radnor command a maid standing nearby.

She hurried away, but Gregory barely took notice of that, in the same way he didn't notice the passage of time that followed. All he could think about was the constables and their words. Someone had provided an anonymous tip that he had come to Ravenmoore to hurt Lady Emma. That couldn't be farther from the truth. He'd met Lady Emma on the first evening of his arrival at Ravenmoore and frankly, didn't consider her anything other than a friend.

The door flew open, and Liana entered the room. She walked straight in his direction, touching his face gently. "Gregory."

He opened his mouth for the first time since Liana's arrival but could not find the words he was searching for. Was this the point where he would be expected to begin telling everyone he was innocent?

There was so much to say, but his throat closed around his words. "They think ..." he managed to murmur.

"I know," she replied quietly, her face frighteningly pale. Her hands trembled, and the sight of her face, full of fear for him, made his heart crumble into bits. He hated seeing her look that way, particularly for his sake.

"Liana, I swear to you ..." he started again.

"I know," Liana repeated, only this time there was an edge to her voice, which Gregory recognized as resoluteness. *She has made up her mind about something. But what?*

He leaned further into her touch, seeking a silent solace. The last time he'd seen her; she was in a floral gown. She had joined him in the Ravenmoore secret garden, where they had spent the entire afternoon in the shade, discussing Liana's favorite books. He'd fed her berries and sweets from the kitchen. Her flowery scent, intermixed with the aroma of the roses, had been intoxicating, enough to linger in his thoughts. He'd known then, just as he had on many other occasions, that he would never be able to let her go again.

Except in this instance, he felt a flush of shame as he sat in front of her. This was quite clearly a set-up, but it still felt embarrassing to be entangled in such a mess. Whomever it was who had orchestrated this scandalous event wished to ruin his reputation and destroy him in front of everyone he loved. One of whom was Liana.

"I don't know what ... where ..." he stammered out, which was quite unlike him. However, in front of Liana, he felt entirely undone.

"You don't have to explain, Gregory."

There it was again. That unplaceable edge in her voice.

"But I have to. This was a deliberate scheme, I promise you. I would never hurt anyone intentionally, let alone Lady Emma."

Liana touched his face again and looked at him with a plea in her eyes. "I know."

Gregory searched her eyes for the truth about how she truly felt. Did she really know, or was she just not ready to talk about it with him? There was something about her tone that caused him to suspect that she was holding back.

"Do you have any idea who it could be?" she inquired gently.

"I have a fair idea, but I'd rather give it a great deal of thought before making any accusations."

Liana nodded after a long pause. It was yet another unusual act that caused him to wonder what she was thinking.

Gregory opened his mouth to speak again, his hands reaching gently for hers. He felt like he was a young boy again, trying to convince the world of his brother's innocence. "You believe me, don't you—"

"I do," she whispered again, but this time her voice cracked. "You don't need to convince me. But someone clearly wants to convince the rest of the world otherwise."

Dora appeared in his line of vision, her face full of concern. "We'll get to the bottom of this, Mr. Holt. Don't you worry. In the meantime, we had best aid the constables in their investigation. Someone at Ravenmoore Estate has nefarious motives, and if we don't seek them out, they just might lead to our ruin."

"Correct," Alex said in agreement. Turning to the officials, he continued. "Gentlemen, I suggest you begin your investigation with the house staff and the guests. Be sure to check the rooms for unusual items of visitors. There's more to this than meets the eye."

The ear-pinching constable nodded, already scribbling in a small notebook.

Dora drew closer to Liana, and Gregory heard her whisper, "Come with me."

"I'll be back shortly," Liana reassured him. Gregory caught a final look of her face before she turned to face Dora. The only way to describe it was that it was full of pure determination. There was no flicker of uncertainty or doubt this time, which was quite unusual for Liana.

As she departed the room with her sister, Gregory couldn't help but remember the last time she had walked away from him. She'd broken the news to him with a strange look on her face, just like this one.

At that time, he had run after her, pleading for an explanation for her actions. This time, he stood at a distance, remembering the ever-fresh feeling of abandonment once again. The thought of Liana leaving him again was too much to bear, and his head hurt from merely thinking about it.

Gregory walked to the far end of the room and stood in silence, his bones rattling due to an unexplainable cold that bit into his skin. He felt a quivering defeat spreading through his limbs.

He no longer felt the need to advocate for his innocence or hope for something more.

Drained of strength, he sank to the ground, giving up.

Chapter Seventeen

A couple of minutes earlier...

Liana had felt like the world suddenly crashed around her. It was like a dam had broken and sound flooded her senses. She heard the rustling of skirts, the shuffling of hurried feet across polished floors, and the growing murmur of voices rising in scattered pockets throughout the estate. The maids were whispering in corners, their words sharp and hurried, laced with fragments of gossip and fear.

"They say she was found in the west garden, barely breathing ..." she heard a lady mutter.

"Lady Emma? Who would do such a thing?"

"I heard that it was poison. And it appears Mr. Holt is a major suspect in this. He's said to be the one who gave her the tea."

Liana barely had time to process any of it. The rumors were spreading faster than she could catch them. The manor's stone walls, old and dignified, now echoed with scandal, and the surrounding shadows seemed to carry the weight of accusation. By the time she made it down the main hallway, the news had already reached most of the manor's occupants and they'd begun forming their own conclusions.

She pushed through the whispers, which were as thick as fog, her thoughts spinning. She had to find Gregory. She had to find Alex. She needed the truth.

Before she could reach the study, a breathless maid appeared in the hallway, nearly colliding with her.

"Miss Liana, the earl is asking for you."

Dora showed up at Liana's side, catching her arm to steady her. "We're on our way," she said briskly, taking charge as she often did when things threatened to spiral.

Liana barely noticed the maid's answering nod. She was still trying to understand what was happening. Just moments ago, she and Dora had been discussing the arrival of the constables at Ravenmoore. Dora had come to her room the moment she heard of it, her face full of information. Something wasn't right, she'd said. Police officials weren't in the habit of visiting Ravenmoore Estate.

"They arrived without warning," Dora had told her. "The constables didn't look like they were here on friendly business."

They soon learned why. Lady Emma had been found unconscious in her room, her skin clammy and her breathing shallow. They found a cup of unfinished tea on her bedside table, and the verdict had been swift: poison.

The kitchen staff and maids had denied serving her tea, and no one knew who had. Yet, with the appearance of the constables, Gregory's name was being spoken in speculative tones. Someone claimed he'd argued with Emma earlier. Another person said he was last spotted with her near the terrace.

"It's a setup," Liana had said in disbelief. "It has to be."

"Of course it is," Dora agreed. "But that doesn't matter in the court of public opinion. Everyone likes to assume they know the facts. People are fascinated by the prospect of a scandal. They don't care about the truth and would rather keep up appearances."

And that was what terrified Liana the most. That Gregory could be harmed or affected due to baseless opinions.

As the three of them hurried down the hallway, Liana had the strange feeling that everything was about to change. If they didn't act quickly, if the real truth wasn't uncovered and Gregory's name cleared, then the manor's legacy would fall under the weight of a lie.

And Gregory, the true love of her life, might never recover from it.

The moment she walked into her brother's study and Gregory looked at her, his eyes begged her to believe him. She had not needed him to plead that. She knew he was incapable of hurting anyone, particularly Lady Emma.

However, she felt a painful tug in her heart. How could Gregory doubt that she believed him? That only showed how deeply he was affected by the unfair accusations cast against him. He'd made several attempts to explain himself, but she found it unnecessary.

Instead, she found herself thinking of how to figure out who framed him and why.

* * *

Now, as she trailed after Dora, she wondered where to begin. The door to the study closed behind her with a soft click, but the sound echoed like thunder in Liana's ears.

She took a shaky breath and turned to Dora. Her sister was standing with her arms crossed and an unreadable expression on her face. She could already tell that whatever Dora was about to say might be unpleasant.

"Liana," Dora said gently. "The situation with Mr. Holt is rather—"

"I'm not leaving him, if that's what you were about to suggest," Liana interrupted loudly. "I won't make such a decision."

"I wasn't about to suggest that," Dora replied, blinking in surprise. "I don't know whether to be proud or upset. This is the first time you've ever raised your voice at me, which is admirable. However, I can't get past your assumption that I would ask you to abandon Gregory Holt."

"I'm sorry for saying that," Liana apologized, blushing in embarrassment. "I just ... I was afraid for a moment there."

"Things will be alright," her sister replied. "No one is abandoning anyone. "I pulled you aside so we could discuss what to do. While the constables focus on their investigations, we need to play our part in finding out who made the false report against Mr. Holt and who gave Lady Emma that tea."

Liana exhaled slowly, some of the tension leaving her shoulders. She glanced down the hallway and at the study, where Gregory was being detained like a criminal.

"That's right. Lady Emma is the only one whose words can free Gregory from these accusations. She has the answers we need. We can't let anything happen to her."

"Do you have a plan?" Dora asked curiously.

"There's an old lady who lives in the village nearby. I've been told that she has an excellent knowledge of poisons and herbs."

"Herbs?"

Liana nodded. "If there's a chance that she can identify the poison given to Lady Emma, then perhaps she can find the right herbs to bring Lady Emma back to a healthy state."

"Are you certain that she'll be of help? Time is of the essence right now."

"A few years ago, I had returned from London to spend a few days at the manor. One of the estate workers had fallen sick from a mysterious illness, and the old lady's help was sought. She treated the estate worker with nothing but crushed herbs and tinctures, but she saved his life."

"I see," Dora replied, nodding in understanding. "So, you'd like to bring her to the manor to come see Lady Emma?"

"Yes. She may be able to aid us in figuring out what was in Lady Emma's tea and in producing the antidote."

A look of relief intermixed with hope entered Dora's eyes. "That would be amazing, Liana."

Liana was hopeful, too. She needed to be, in order to accomplish her goal of saving Gregory.

"That look ... you intend to fetch her yourself, don't you?"

Liana nodded. "Right now, in fact. I don't trust anyone else to fetch her as quickly."

"Then go," Dora encouraged. "We'll take care of things in your absence."

Without wasting another minute, Liana hugged her sister and hurried away without sparing anyone another word. She made her way through the manor with hasty steps, stopping only when she arrived at the stables.

She saddled her mare with swift, practiced hands. The stable boy rushed forward, his eyes wide in surprise.

"Shall I prepare a carriage, my lady?"

"There's no time," Liana said, mounting the house in one graceful motion. "There's no need to raise any alarm. I'll return shortly."

She didn't wait for a response. The wind tore through her hair and cloak as she rode hard through the winding lanes, the mare's hooves pounding like war drums against the packed earth. It was a cold, windy day, and the signs of a storm brewing were in the air.

There was a rising fear within her. She could feel it trying to make its way across her insides, but the fire within her heart burned hotter. Gregory's face filled her thoughts again. There was the disbelief in his eyes and the way his shoulders had slumped seconds before she left the study.

She hadn't told him then, but she would now.

She was going to save him. This time, she wasn't about to let him go.

After a considerable amount of time spent on horseback, Liana arrived at the familiar terrain of the village. Soon, the herb lady's cottage came into view. It was small and half-hidden behind tangled ivy and blooming chamomile.

She was home, Liana realized with a relieved smile. Smoke curled from the chimney, a comforting sight. The old lady was likely brewing herbs or a healing concoction, and all Liana knew was that being present at the village brought her a feeling of calmness.

Liana dismounted from the horse, made her way to the door and knocked with urgency.

The door revealed a weathered woman in a faded shawl. She looked older than Liana recalled, but her eyes remained the same. They were as bright as shimmering glass.

"Lady Liana?" The herb woman asked in surprise. It was not common to see a lady of Liana's status riding alone to speak to a villager. Anyone who saw her had to have known the situation was dire.

"There's no time," Liana managed to say, attempting to gather her composure after a lengthy ride. "A woman at the manor has been poisoned. We need you."

"Very well," the older lady said. Liana admired her lack of hesitation and quick understanding that there was trouble, and none but her could resolve it.

The herb lady turned back into her home, gathering satchels and bundles of dried herbs with quick efficiency.

"Is there anything peculiar about her situation?" She asked quickly as she maneuvered around the cottage, picking up one thing or the other.

"All we know is that she drank a tea that was infused with something unhealthy. We kept the cup."

"And her current state?"

"Barely breathing. She's been unconscious since ingesting the tea."

"Hm," the herb lady said, as if realizing something.

She walked to another corner, gathering more dried herbs. After that, she turned to Liana.

"We're ready. Let's go."

"I hope you're fine with riding with me," Liana said, walking toward her horse.

The herb lady nodded and, with Liana's help, mounted the horse. In the next minute, they rode along the route to the manor at rapid speed.

* * *

They arrived just after dusk. The manor loomed above in the twilight shadow, and the sight of it seemed hopeful and negative at the same time. Liana and the healer strode through the doors, ignoring questioning looks from the footmen and maids. The rest of the household, guests included, seemed to be elsewhere, perhaps at dinner or some other event. Liana had the feeling Alex had organized a function to distract people from recent events.

"Where's she?" The herb lady muttered as they hurried along the hallways.

"Upstairs," Liana replied. "I'll take you."

Their journey continued in silence, except for the sound of their footsteps. Soon, they arrived at Lady Emma's chambers.

"I already have an idea of what she was poisoned with," the herb lady commented with a sniffle. "But I intend to confirm my suspicions when we're inside."

Liana's heart rose with hope at the statement. Perhaps there was a chance that Lady Emma would be saved.

They entered the room to find Lady Emma's maid in a corner, anxiously wringing her hands.

"I found someone who can be of help," Liana said to the maid, who looked relieved at their arrival. "Please find Dora and bring her here."

The maid nodded and rushed out of the room. Liana watched as the herb lady moved to stand beside Lady Emma. She felt the lady's pale skin with a contemplative look on her face. Next, she sniffed the sweat on her skin before checking her breathing with a well-placed finger in front of her nose. Nodding in some kind of awareness, she took a glance at the teacup next to the bed.

Then she went back to her bag, filled with satchels and dried herbs, and began sorting through them.

The maid had returned with Dora, who now stood in a corner, watching the herb lady work.

"I need boiled water, fresh linens, garlic, crushed chamomile, and honey," the herb lady said without glancing up. "In the next ten minutes, preferably."

"I shall make arrangements for that," the maid replied, departing from the room hurriedly.

The herb lady picked out some herbs of choice and began crushing them together. Liana wished she understood what the process meant, but mere observation of the herb lady's actions provided little clarity. All she had now was hope. Hope that the older woman would be able to heal Emma.

"You did well, Liana," Dora whispered, placing a gentle hand on her back. "You got her here in time."

Not quite knowing what to say in reply, Liana managed a faint smile. Her eyes remained fixed on the figure lying unconscious on the bed. "I hope it was enough," she said quietly. "I hope she saves her."

"She will," Dora replied, her voice firm despite a slight tremor. "She has to."

The door creaked open as the maid returned, her arms filled with linens, vials, and a basin of water. She looked as shaken as everyone else in the room. The healer took the vials and began mixing them into the crushed herbs, her hands steady despite the tension in the air.

"You don't have to worry about Gregory," Dora continued softly. "He won't be going anywhere. Alexander has made certain of that. He has considerable influence in the courts and the House of Lords. Moreover, he's made significant donations to the police force for several years now and has political sway. The constables have agreed to keep Gregory at the manor until his innocence or guilt is determined."

"That's a relief," Liana murmured with a bit of joy. She'd been worried that the constables would take Gregory away in her absence. "I can't wait until he's back outside, innocent and free of accusation."

"Given your efforts, I'm certain that will happen sooner rather than later," Dora replied. "This summer has been a rather eventful one. I'll never again complain about having to remain at the manor for the entire summer."

Liana managed a tiny, sad smile, knowing how stubborn her sister could get. "You will."

Dora returned the smile. "Oh, you know I will. In the meantime, don't bother about anything else. We'll look after Lady Emma together."

Liana stepped closer to the bed. The herb woman had poured some of the mix she'd created down Lady Emma's throat. Now she was murmuring to herself, her hands moving expertly over Lady Emma's wrist. She felt for a pulse, then checked her breathing. The older woman pulled a vial from her satchel and uncorked it, letting the scent drift under Lady Emma's nose.

"She's breathing," the healer muttered. "But only just. It's a good thing you fetched me in time."

Liana felt a squeezing in her chest. "Will she make it?"

The healer didn't answer, her brow furrowed in concentration. Liana stood motionless at the foot of the bed, her arms hanging at her side. Every second dragged like an hour. Lady Emma's chest barely moved. Her skin was pale, too pale. But she was alive.

Her current state was a far cry from the charming lady who had spoken with Liana in the garden. That lady had been nice to talk to and in good health.

"She has to live," Liana whispered, more to herself than anyone else.

"She will," Dora said again, but this time her voice broke slightly.

"Their lives are quite interlinked, these two amazing individuals. Gregory and Emma," Liana said with a cracked voice. "If she dies, they'll hang Gregory. Watching her in this state is incredibly scary."

Dora said nothing, but she didn't have to. Her eyes held a great deal of concern as well.

The healer broke the silence. "This will be difficult, but she has a chance. Keep her warm, and let's see what occurs."

Liana clenched her fists. A chance. That was all she needed.

"I won't let either of them die," she whispered, carefully placing a blanket over Emma. "I'll do whatever it takes."

Chapter Eighteen

The morning light slipped quietly through the tall windows of the manor, casting a soft hue over the eastern wing where Gregory's chambers lay. He was being detained there until some conclusion could be drawn regarding Lady Emma. The household was yet to awaken fully. Most people were drowsy from the unrest of the previous night, still tiptoeing around the weight of scandal.

Liana stood outside his door for longer than she should. Her fingers hovered near the brass door handle. She kept her breathing measured in an attempt to remain steady in appearance while cracking beneath the surface. She had rehearsed what to say a dozen times. But now, with the door in front of her and the man she loved dearly alone on the other side, the words felt like dust in her mouth.

She knocked gently. There was a pause, followed by the sound of slow, deliberate footsteps.

The door creaked open, and Gregory appeared, still in the clothes from the previous day, although his tailcoat was gone and his collar was undone. His eyes were rimmed with fatigue, the sort that a night's sleep couldn't fix. It was the sort of look that came from betrayal. Or worse, disbelief that the people you once trusted might now look at you with doubt.

"Liana," he muttered in a raw voice.

"I just ..." she swallowed, forcing her spine straighter. "I wanted to see you."

Wordlessly, he stepped aside for her to come in, and she did so. The room was dim, and the curtains were half drawn. A plate of untouched breakfast sat on the side table. Books were stacked haphazardly by the hearth, but the fire was out. The air was rife with raw nerves, like the silence hanging between them.

She turned to face him, her eyes filled with concern for this man whom she loved most in the world. There was only exhaustion to be found on his face, accompanied by a hollow strength that had always made Gregory seem older than he was.

"This is all news to me," he said quietly. "The scheme to poison Lady Emma."

"I know," she whispered. "It's ridiculous, to say the least."

"Those sergeants ... they looked at me like I was a lost cause."

"You're not," Liana replied fiercely.

He gave a short, humorless laugh. "The footman who brought my meal stood a little farther from me this morning. Another of the maids wouldn't meet my eyes. Now I know what Russell felt during the course of his trial."

At the mention of his brother, Liana noticed that he seemed to deflate even more. "Should I write to Russell? I believe he would be devastated to learn what has happened here. You need more support."

"I already have enough support from you. Don't I?" Gregory asked, his eyes prompting her for a response. Something about his fixed look told her he was eagerly expecting her answer.

"You do," Liana replied with certainty. "You'll never have to worry about where I stand, because I will always be in support. You're not the attacker."

"How can you be sure?"

"Because I know you," she said in a louder voice, pushing through the tightness in her chest. "Because I've seen how noble and kind-hearted you can be. You're a man with strong values who has worked hard to build a better life for himself, despite the odds."

He turned away with a softening expression, and it suddenly looked like multiple weights had been lifted off of him. "I'm glad you're here, Liana. Navigating this would be impossible without you. But I'm afraid none of your generous statements will matter to the world. Evidence, not loyalty, decides guilt. And we both know someone wishes for me to take the fall."

Liana drew closer and took his hand in hers. "Everything will be alright, I promise."

"I'm not so sure about everything, but I'm beyond pleased to have you by my side. The other day, I ..."

"You?" She prompted, waiting for him to continue.

"I was afraid that you had left me. For good."

"That will never happen," Liana replied with a fierceness that seemed to have stunned him. "I lost you once, and I refuse to do so again."

Aware that Gregory was looking at her in astonishment, Liana pressed her lips against his in a quick kiss before leaving the room.

As she walked along the hallway, she felt a flash of anticipation pulsing through her veins. The truth was, the quiet, timid lady he'd grown accustomed to was gone, replaced by a woman who was determined to reach her goals. The events of the past day had elevated her to a better version of herself, and she was resolute about making the best of it.

* * *

In the silence that followed, Gregory stared at the shut door, his chest rising and falling with slow, deliberate breaths. Her presence had stirred warmth, promise, love, hope, and a mix of other positive emotions within him. When she appeared, the tight coil of dread that had taken residence in his gut since the night before loosened.

Liana believed in him, particularly in a time like this. There was no certainty of his innocence, no determined conclusions. And yet she believed in him. Despite his situation, the fact of that left him feeling like the happiest person in the world.

She'd told him everything would be alright in a confident tone.

But what did that mean?

She hasn't made promises of seeking justice or named anyone in particular. Yet, there was something about her tone that led him to suspect there was more. Liana was typically measured with her emotions, always one step ahead of her feelings. But this morning, something within her seemed to have changed. She was on the cusp of something. But then, so was he.

Gregory stared at the closed door, half-expecting her to return. She didn't. Instead, a heavier knock came shortly after. It was sharp and controlled, just like Radnor.

"Well, come in," Gregory said with a severe hint of irony. He couldn't leave the room anyway, and by extension, couldn't grant permission for anyone to enter. But he appreciated that the appearance of free will was being kept at the very least.

Alex walked in, and from the strain around his otherwise sharp eyes, it was obvious that he, too, hadn't gotten much sleep during the night.

There was always a calculated elegance to him, but today it felt more like a profound exhaustion.

It was clear that he wasn't the only one overcome by the recent events. The Foxworth family had shown themselves to be worthy allies through thick and thin.

"You ought to have remained in bed," Gregory said dryly. "Little has altered, I'm afraid."

"I rose early to aid the constables in their investigations," Alex explained, drawing the curtains apart to let in some light. "I've instructed the staff to cooperate fully and answer any questions posed to them. That way, we can get to the bottom of this sooner. In the meantime, I have arranged several events to keep the guests busy," he paused to massage his brow with a frown. "At this rate, Ravenmoore Estate stands to lose its standing as a reputable venue to spend one's summer."

"I'm sorry for bringing this upon you and your family," Gregory said quietly.

"What nonsense," Alex responded, huffing in dismissal. "You're an accomplished businessman, just like the dozens of other businessmen I have invited to my ancestral home on a yearly basis. You're also one of my closest friends. As someone privy to the state of your morals, I refuse to stand by and let you bear the weight of such false accusations."

"I have a fair idea of who's done this," Gregory said, his heart swelling with appreciation at his friend's words. "Also, if I ever get out of this, I promise to join others in spreading the word of Ravenmoore Estate as a delightful destination."

Alex chuckled at that. "There's no need for such measures. The beauty and expansiveness of Ravenmoore Estate are rivalled only by a few. I predict lords, ladies, businessmen, and others will continue to show up here for a long time," he stated before his face turned serious. "Now let's return to the topic of the person you suspect."

"It's none other than my uncle. As you well know, he's a scheming man who will stop at nothing to accomplish his selfish aims. He attempted to ruin my brother's life. There's enough reason to think that he's doing the same to me."

"You make a compelling argument," Alex said. "Whatever happened to that investigator you hired? Surely, he ought to have found enough damning evidence against your uncle by now."

Gregory sighed. He had been wondering the same. "Unfortunately, I have no idea. I would not be surprised to learn that the poor investigator found little to incriminate my uncle. He's a rather wily man."

"His reign of terror will end soon," Alex stated matter-of-factly. "I'll send word to the division head of the London Police to see if we can discover the identity of the anonymous tip. In the meantime, we need to discover the perpetrator among us."

"Whoever did it definitely knew the right time to pick for their nefarious act," Gregory noted. "Giving Lady Emma a cup of tea at dawn, when there were no witnesses present, was very calculated. I was in bed at the time, leaving me with no alibi and no way to protest the allegations levelled against me."

Alex placed a supporting hand on his shoulder. "We'll find that person. I spotted Liana leaving the room minutes before my arrival. I hope things are alright between you two."

It was unusual for Alex to interfere in his and Liana's affairs, but having witnessed how dejected Gregory looked the previous day, his concern was understandable. "Things are perfect, in fact. She may not know it, but having her by my side through this has helped me in more ways than one."

Alex looked speculative. "She's been acting differently."

Gregory nodded. "I know what you mean. The change isn't anything particularly great, but it's subtle enough to be noticed. She's more ... intent."

"And focused," Alex added. "It's like something in her snapped into place. I don't know what she's up to, but I have never seen her like this. Early this morning, she sent out a message through one of the horse riders. I only found out because I overheard the stable hand complaining about the lack of warning."

"Did she say anything in particular to you?"

"Not at all," Alex responded. "All my life, I have always known Liana to be kind and helpful. I'm certain whatever she's doing can't be entirely terrible, but I also wonder why she's being so secretive about it."

"Yesterday, she rode down to the village to find a healer for Lady Emma. I do not yet know what the result of that is, but I do hope that it's helpful."

That drew more of Gregory's attention. "Do you think the healer can succeed in aiding Lady Emma's recovery?"

"From the look of things, she's incredibly capable. But we'll only know for certain by the end of the day," Alex said.

"Although I'm grateful and awed by Liana's efforts, I can't help worrying about her. She seems to be straining herself," Gregory shared.

"She loves you. It's what anyone in the same situation would do."

Gregory exhaled, his unease stirring again. "If she's digging around and acting in secret, does this mean she suspects someone?"

"Perhaps so. I presume you've already told her about your uncle?"

"Yes. Should I not have?"

"No, it's alright. I'm glad you shared that information as well. Secrets are never good for a long-term union, after all," the earl said. "In any case, Liana's involvement isn't to be frowned upon. We need all hands available."

"That may be true, but I don't want her exhausted—"

"She won't be," Alex promised. "As her older brother, I'll ensure that she gets enough rest."

"Thank you."

"Thank me after all of this is over," Alex replied with a dismissive wave. "Right now, every aristocratic house from here to Merrowbrook will have heard whispers about what has occurred. Lady Emma's family will expect to learn more about the state of their daughter. I have already sent out a letter explaining everything, but I expect there will be regular correspondence to keep them informed."

"And? I'm sensing there's more."

"And if we don't arrive at the end of this quickly, the courts will call for an official inquiry. That will mean a trial, more questioning, and perhaps Lady Emma's family getting involved."

Gregory sank into the chair by the hearth, dragging a hand through his hair. "If Emma dies—"

"She won't," Alex cut in quickly. "I don't know so much about the healer, but I have no other choice but to believe she'll help the lady recover."

"It might be best to assign a guard or footman to accompany Liana everywhere she goes," Gregory suggested. "If the killer is still here at Ravenmoore, they may not appreciate being investigated and will likely do anything to avoid being found out."

"That's an excellent idea. I'll be sure to install someone next to her at all times."

Gregory nodded in satisfaction, then paused. The past few hours had been so intense that he had not had enough time to consider how the poison would affect Lady Emma once she awoke. She would be terrified to learn someone had tried to murder her by handing her tea. Would she conceive a dislike for tea afterwards? Or to Ravenmoore Estate? If she did, he would not begrudge her for that.

"Do you think she'll take the news of being poisoned well?"

"Lady Emma? I predict she will likely be somewhat disturbed, but otherwise unharmed," Alex answered, approaching a small table near the hearth and pouring himself a glass of water. "She's a lady of the court, Gregory. Raised in suspicion and taught to maintain her composure, especially in dire situations. Contrary to popular opinion, one does not survive the inner circles without a near-death experience or the other."

Something in Radnor's tone told Gregory he was also referring to something private, which may have occurred in his life as well. In another time, he would have considered pressing for more information, but this time he chose to let things be.

"Liana was raised in a similarly elite family, but she doesn't strike me as matching the description you've provided."

"I'm sure Liana must have told you this already, but she and Dora didn't grow up in court or high society," Alex explained. "While I stayed with my father and spent my childhood at Ravenmoore Estate and in London, my sisters spent a large chunk of their upbringing in the northern cottage my mother occupied until her death."

Gregory nodded. Liana had, in fact, told him that. In a way, the differences in how they had been raised explained the personalities of both women. Liana was generous to a fault and innocent regarding the ways of life, whereas Dora was outspoken and quick to laugh. Such distinct identities were a contrast to traditional ladies raised in court or high society, who were often strait-laced and too conscious of their dresses or smiles to come across as anything other than bland.

"In any case," Alex continued after taking a long sip of water. "Whoever has harmed Lady Emma wants chaos. Not a quiet disappearance—a spectacle. A scandal. One that ensures your name is dragged through the mud and strikes at Ravenmoore Estate's reputation."

"It's rather cowardly and pathetic to attack a man without showing one's face," Gregory said disgustedly.

"I agree with that sentiment," Alex said, setting down the glass. "Brave men step forward and express their dissatisfaction publicly. Cowards hide in the shadows, scheming and plotting. But I assure you, in this case, they will not succeed."

Before Gregory could reply, the door swung open. Liana walked in, her cloak still clinging to her shoulders, damp from the morning fog. Her eyes were brighter than they had been earlier—sharp and glowing with what seemed like a vibrant shade of hope.

"She's awake," Liana announced.

Gregory's breath halted momentarily. "Lady Emma?"

Liana nodded. "She opened her eyes only a couple of minutes ago. As soon as I had confirmed the state of her health, I left to inform you of the news. It might be best for us to depart now and visit her together."

"Is she alright?" Gregory asked.

"She's weak. Still pale," Liana answered. "But she's lucid. The healer thinks the worst has passed."

Alex exhaled slowly, relief flickering across his face. "That changes things."

"Yes," Liana agreed, a happy smile playing on her lips. "It changes everything."

Daring to hope, Gregory's heartbeat sped a bit faster. "Did she say anything about what happened?"

"Only fragments," Liana replied, her smile disappearing. "She recalls the tea. The sharp pain before falling unconscious. The bitter taste. But she doesn't remember who brought it to her."

Alexander frowned. "Then we're still blind."

"Not entirely," Liana said, stepping closer. "She said something else just before I left her bedside."

"What was it?" Gregory asked.

"She said she saw gold. She added that her last memory of you was from weeks ago, when you were partnered with her at the ball."

"Gold?"

Liana nodded. "Precisely, and not in a painted way. She described it as a glint at the tip of his index finger, like metal catching light."

"However strange the description might sound, it at least clarifies that the attacker could not have been Gregory," Alexander pointed out. "But it's not sufficient enough to hold in court."

"No," she replied in agreement. "But it's certainly something. Moreover, it means that she saw something before she lost consciousness. She wasn't entirely unaware."

"Can we see her?" Gregory asked.

"Yes. It's why I came to fetch you, after all. But be careful, she's fragile and scared."

"Before we go ahead," Alex began. "I'd like to ask if you're alright. You haven't had much rest in recent days, have you?"

"No, I haven't," Liana replied. "But I expect that will change as soon as this matter is resolved."

"Did you get any sleep last night at least?" Gregory asked, his voice filled with worry.

"I didn't," she admitted, fixing him a warm smile. "I think I'll only ever get to do that again when you're safe and free."

Something within Gregory soared. It was a mixture of many things, but the most distinct part was a brimming sense of love. Love for this woman who cared for him just as much or even more than herself.

"That time will come soon enough," Gregory replied confidently, drawing another smile from Liana.

Alex cleared his throat loudly, but there was a faint smile playing on his lips. "We had best get going."

Gregory nodded. He held his hand out, and Liana took it. Together, they walked out of the room, stepping into a future filled with prospects.

Chapter Nineteen

They headed down the long hallway, the sound of their footsteps echoing the uncertainty that gripped them. Liana led the way, her posture straight and her stride swift. Gregory followed closely behind, flanked by Alexander, Dora, and the two constables. Sunlight filtered through the tall windows, spilling fractured light onto the polished floors and casting long shadows on the stone walls.

Gregory's gaze rested on Liana's back as she walked. He was in awe of the woman blossoming before him in a manner akin to flowers in spring. Something about her had changed. She walked with renewed purpose, her head held high and a fierce energy radiating from her with every step. Despite the fatigue in her eyes, she moved like someone who had made a plan and was determined to make it a reality.

"She's blazing with fire," Gregory murmured under his breath.

Alex turned to him with a knowing look. "She always burns the brightest when she's protecting those she loves. The most mild-tempered individuals have been known to lead the battle when there's something worth fighting for. In this case, that means you."

Gregory gave no reply, but Radnor's words hit as deep as a skillfully released arrow. He would always love Liana in all her aspects. He loved her when she was shy and quiet, and he especially loved the protective side of her, which seemed to show up whenever he was in trouble.

Liana paused outside the ornate door to Lady Emma's chamber before pushing it open with calm authority. The scent of herbs, soap, and old wood lingered in the air. The healer was adjusting a blanket at the edge of the bed but stepped aside as they entered.

Lady Emma was sitting upright now, propped by pillows. She looked frail but alert, her skin still pale but no longer ghost-like. Her eyes, once clouded with fever and exhaustion, were now sharp with recognition.

"Lady Emma," Liana called, her voice soft. "These guests have come to converse with you. Are you prepared?"

"I am," Lady Emma replied with a single nod. "My memory ... it's clearer now."

Gregory stepped forward, picking his words carefully to keep her from being overwhelmed. "I'm glad to see you in a better state of health. Could you please tell us what happened before you lost consciousness?"

Her gaze shifted slowly to him. "Thank you, Mr. Holt. I remember being served a warm drink. An herbal tea. I thought it had been prepared by Bertha, my personal maid. But the person who brought the tea to me wasn't Bertha."

"Who was it? One of the constables asked.

"A male servant. He said Bertha had been briefly called away and he was sent in her place. I had never seen him before."

"Are you certain he wasn't a member of the household staff?" the other constable asked.

"Quite sure. He was unfamiliar. Blond hair, average height, and clean-shaven. And there was the gold tip of his finger, which I already mentioned. I asked his name, but he only smiled and told me he was here temporarily."

"And then you drank the tea?" Gregory asked gently.

Lady Emma nodded. "Yes. Within minutes, I felt ... odd. My limbs went heavy. My thoughts clouded, and I tried to stand but couldn't. Everything spun ... and then nothing."

The first constable turned to Gregory with narrowed eyes. "That sounds like a classic sedative. This was definitely planned."

"And could have been ordered by someone with access to the household," added the second officer, his voice laced with accusation. "Someone like you, Mr. Holt."

Gregory stiffened. "There's no tangible evidence to suggest I was involved in this."

The second constable shrugged. "You benefit the most if she's out of the way."

"How so?" Lady Emma enquired in confusion, looking appalled. "You're of the assumption that Mr. Holt tried to poison me? That would be ridiculous."

Before the argument could escalate further, the door burst open and one of Radnor's guards strode in, dragging a young man by the arm.

"I caught him sneaking through the east corridor, heading toward the servants' exit," the guard announced. "We do not recognize him as a working member of this household. Moreover, he was acting furtively."

The entire room went quiet as they all glanced in the direction of the young man. He was an exact representation of Lady Emma's description.

THE GENTLEMAN'S BETROTHAL   189

"He is blonde and clean-shaven, just like Lady Emma said," one of the maids exclaimed, announcing what everyone else was thinking.

"That's certainly strange," the first constable said.

"I gave instructions for anyone seen trying to leave to be seized," Alex announced.

The man the guard had restrained was slight, with a mop of tousled blond hair and a look of panic across his face. His kitchen uniform was stained and torn, as though he'd been running through the hedges.

Gregory's stomach twisted in awareness. "I've seen him before," he said aloud.

"Where?" Liana asked curiously.

"On Ravenmoore grounds. During a picnic event that occurred a few weeks ago. He was dressed as a footman, and I thought he looked rather peculiar. I inquired into his identity and was told that his name was Will, and that he was a new employee at Ravenmoore."

The young man struggled against the guard's grip, his gaze darting around the room like a trapped animal.

Lady Emma sat up straighter in bed, her voice growing firm. "That's him. He's the one who gave me the drink."

"And the golden tip of his finger?" One of the constables asked skeptically.

Alex walked to the man and took his gloves off. "Here it is," he said, lifting the man's bare hand, where a golden contraption had been fitted at the tip of his finger. "The glint of gold Lady Emma noticed."

"He likely lost a part of his finger in an injury and replaced it with a gold piece," Liana said. "It's a process common in certain parts of the world and has clearly been replicated here."

"What's your name?" Alex questioned.

The man said nothing.

"You'll speak now," one of the constables snapped, stepping forward. "Or we'll assume you were sent by Mr. Holt and act accordingly."

"No," Liana interjected. "He speaks for himself, not for Gregory. We'll determine the extent of his actions individually."

"I'll have you know that it is in your best interest to tell the truth," Gregory said sternly. "You have no way of getting out of this otherwise."

"I think we should leave the room. Now that we have a suspect, we can let Lady Emma rest," Dora suggested.

On everyone's agreement, the guards removed the man from the room. But the room had barely settled after the man's removal when another guard returned, sounding slightly out of breath.

"He's talking," the guard said, glancing at Alex and Gregory. "He began confessing once he was secured in the left wing study. I think it's beginning to dawn on him that there's no escape route."

"In that case, we'll all go to hear what he has to say," Gregory said.

Minutes later, they all gathered in the study. It was a warm room lined with books, and a fireplace flickered in the corner. The man sat on a wooden chair with his wrists bound and his shoulders hunched like a collapsed umbrella. He looked up briefly as Gregory, Liana, and Alex approached. The two constables were also present, standing quietly next to the door.

"I don't know why I'm doing this," the young man muttered. "It's not like it will change anything."

"You can't have been acting independently," Liana said to him. "Who sent you?"

The man licked his lips, eyes darting to Gregory, then back down to the floor. "I shouldn't be saying anything ... but what's the point in protecting him anymore?"

Alex leaned forward. "Who?"

"My father," the man replied in a low but steady voice. "My name is Ebenezer. The name Will was only an alias."

"And who are you truly, Ebenezer?" Gregory asked.

"I am the bastard son of Lord Osborne."

A thick silence fell before Gregory broke it. "Osborne?" he repeated, as a wave of realization dawned on him. "That's my uncle, is it not?"

Ebenezer nodded once. "He met my mother whilst on a trip to London. She was a lowly commoner, and he was a high lord, which made the possibility of raising me publicly very unlikely. Instead, he sent monthly allowances to my mother and visited occasionally. Each time, he would tell me stories regarding what was stolen from him by your father ... and then by you."

Liana's lips parted in surprise. "He's your cousin?"

"Illegitimate cousin," Gregory corrected bitterly. "I didn't even know he existed."

"I didn't exist to your family," Ebenezer spat, his eyes filled with hatred. "Not until Lord Osborne found a use for me."

He exhaled deeply, as though years of resentment were escaping in one breath. "He promised me a future. Respect and recognition. He told me all I had to do was aid him in destroying your reputation. He hoped to accomplish that by framing you for something that would bury you in prison or lead to scandal, just as he did to your brother."

"My brother almost didn't recover from that scandal," Gregory said through clenched teeth. "He was arrested and exiled from the family home."

"That was Lord Osborne's doing?" Dora asked from her position next to Radnor.

Ebenezer nodded. "He wanted complete access and control of your father's estate. Your brother resisted, refusing to let that happen. So, Lord Osborne changed the course of events. He orchestrated a disgrace that would not only subdue Russell but prevent anyone else from considering him a man of substance."

"And you were supposed to do the same to me," Gregory said.

"Yes," Ebenezer murmured. "Lady Emma was only a small part of a bigger plan. I picked her because of her title and family influence, figuring that would garner more public attention. Whilst I was here in Ravenmoore carrying out my plan, Lord Osborne arranged for the police to receive a report about Gregory Holt's planned attack on Lady Emma. The expectation was that she'd be dead upon their arrival and Holt would be taken into custody."

Liana's hand shot to her mouth in surprise. "How awful ..."

"He despises you," Evenezer continued, looking directly at Gregory. "Everything about you, in fact. He called you the golden heir. He said that you wore honor like an untouched cloak, but your clean record was a fluke, waiting to be broken."

Alex crossed his arms. "What did he promise you for this?"

"A title," Ebenezer said, laughing bitterly. "A name. He said if I brought you down, he'd petition the courts to recognize me officially. He'd also give me a stretch of fertile land and access to a better future."

"You'd trade a woman's life for a name?" Dora asked sharply.

A cruel glint appeared in Ebenezer's eyes. "I would do anything for a better life."

"Had you come to me, I would have arranged that for you without any expectations," Gregory responded. "It's a shame you took this path instead."

Ebenezer fell quiet, seeming to consider the statement. "I'm not an adventurous man. Even if you had offered that, I would still have taken Lord Osborne's offer. He's my father, after all."

The two officers exchanged looks, then stepped forward.

"Enough," one of them said. "You'll write down everything you've just confessed. We'll investigate Lord Osborne's involvement separately, but this ... this is more than enough to clear Mr. Holt's name from the poisoning incident."

"And then what?" Ebenezer asked bitterly. "Back to the slums? I was born in the shadows, raised in it ... and now it appears I'll die there too."

"No," Gregory said quietly, fixing his steely gaze on the younger man. "You'll live. That's worse for men like you and Osborne. You'll watch as we untangle his schemes. I'll make sure every title he's clung to gets stripped piece by piece."

Ebenezer gave no reply and looked away in clear defiance. He was taken away shortly after, shackled not only by iron, but by the weight of the truth he was made to unveil. The police carriage wheels squealed loudly over gravel before fading into the night. The crowd of maids, guards, and a few guests dispersed, and the study was quiet except for the fire's quiet crackle.

Liana approached Gregory slowly. "Are you alright?"

He shook his head. "Not quite. But I'm glad to know the truth. I always suspected Osborne had something to do with what happened to Russell. But this? This is the height of criminality."

Alex placed a supportive hand on Gregory's shoulder. "Well, you have us now. We'll support you as you dismantle his power piece by piece."

Gregory's heart swelled with love for the woman he cared the most for in the world and her equally endearing family. Life had made up for his uncle's villainous behaviour by granting him the love of others. It was more than he could ever hope for.

He nodded gratefully. "That's relieving to hear. I need to write to my brother and inform him that our hunch was correct. What happened to him wasn't coincidental. It was a deliberate scheme meant to lead him into ruin."

"I'm certain he'd be immensely validated by that information," Liana said with a warm smile.

"He definitely would be," Gregory responded, in awe of the woman he'd fallen in love with. She was a beacon of softness and strength, the two combining in a brilliant mix.

The manor and its occupants had collectively taken a deep exhale. The maids were resuming their duties, guards returning to their posts, and whispers of the ordeal were tapering into silence.

Alex cleared his throat. "It's been a long day, and we had best head to dinner."

"The events of the day left me so astounded, I was tongue-tied," Dora added, stretching her limbs. "I hope to make up for it by roping an innocent lady or gentleman into a heated conversation."

They all left the study, their voices echoing along the hallway. But as Alex and Dora went ahead, Gregory paused and took Liana's hand. For a long moment, neither of them spoke. The candlelight from the sconces flickered across Liana's face, highlighting the outline of her cheekbones and bow-tipped lips.

"Somewhere through this ordeal, I thought I lost you," he divulged in a hoarse voice. "I'm glad that isn't the case. I cannot imagine this victory without you present."

"You will never have to imagine that, Gregory," Liana murmured, her eyes welling up with joyful tears. "I am so glad you're free. I'm sorry for giving the impression that I was leaving you. I was much too taken by the idea of resolving the situation to provide more reassurance."

"Don't blame yourself," he said, shaking his head. "After realizing you weren't leaving me, I was too impressed by your determination to consider anything else."

Liana smiled. "I was rather determined, wasn't I? I have never felt so motivated to right the wrongs. I suppose this is a good thing to learn about oneself."

"That you'll fight hard for me?"

"Yes," Liana replied, drawing closer. "And that you are my source of strength."

"I could say the same. Frankly, I was on the far end of my sanity until you visited in the morning."

"Then I'm glad to have intervened before things got worse," Liana murmured. "I choose you, Gregory. I'll always choose you."

"And I'm choosing you," he whispered, closing the distance between them. He pressed a soft, chaste kiss on her forehead and hugged her tight before drawing away. A happy tear fell down Liana's face, and he wiped it with his index finger. "No more tears. There's only joy to look forward to henceforth."

"I like the sound of that very much," Liana admitted.

"I'd hoped you would," he said, taking her hand again. "I love you."

"I love you too," she responded, blushing furiously.

"Thank you for saving my life and Lady Emma's," he added.

She ducked her head shyly with a proud smile on her face.

He pulled back just enough to look into her eyes, his thumb brushing a strand of hair from her face. "Liana ..."

"Yes?"

"Marry me," Gregory said, his voice steady but full of emotion. "Not because it's expected or because of duty. Marry me because I cannot imagine another day, another night, another battle, another victory, without you."

Tears shimmered in Liana's eyes, but they did not fall. Instead, she laughed—a soft, joyful laugh that rang like wind chimes on a summer morning.

"You wonderful man," she said, her eyes bright with amazement. "Yes. A thousand times yes!"

"Good," Gregory said and pressed another kiss on her forehead. "We have an immensely blissful life ahead of us."

Chapter Twenty

The morning sun shone brightly, reflecting the mood of those who gathered outside the manor to bid Gregory farewell. Liana had hoped to spend more time with him before their wedding, but the matter with Gregory's uncle had to be resolved completely. That meant traveling to London and lodging in his brother's home while the constables carried out their investigations and brought Lord Osborne to book. She would miss Gregory greatly, that much was for certain, but with the threat of his uncle no longer hovering over them, they'd be better off.

Still, that logical conclusion couldn't keep a lone tear from falling down her cheek. She hated to be apart from him. It was a little pitiful, this reliance she'd come to have on Gregory, but she had never been the sort to value independence above all. That was Dora's preference, not hers. Since meeting Gregory on that fateful day four years ago, all she'd wanted to do was linger in his presence and be the recipient of his love.

As if reading her thoughts, Gregory wiped her tear with his finger and caressed the spot gently. "I'll be back before you know it, Ana."

Ana. The nickname he'd chosen as a medium to further express his affection for her. Hearing him say it with such care filled her with a special sort of giddiness.

"Take care of yourself in London," she murmured with a sniffle. "If I learn that you got hurt or sick, I'll travel there myself."

That drew a chuckle from Gregory. "Somehow, I believe you would do exactly that. The recently concluded events have proven such."

Liana smiled. "I'm glad I can inspire such faith, Gregory Holt."

"Enough, you lovebirds," Dora said in mock disgust, although the wide grin on her face said otherwise. "He'll return before we know it, and then we'll have to endure more of this."

"Not if they move to the manor Gregory plans to build on his family's land," Alexander responded with a smile of his own. "I'll miss Liana greatly, but at least we'll be free of the sappiness."

"Unfortunately, that won't be the case," Gregory told them. "I do not intend to keep Liana from the family she loves dearly, so we intend to visit regularly."

"We'll be sure to lodge you two in our most solitary quarters," Dora said with a mock shudder. "We can do that, can't we?" She asked, turning to Alexander.

The earl's eyes glinted in mischief. "That can certainly be arranged."

Around them, the carriage was being loaded by footmen, and Gregory's travel bag was properly secured.

"I'll be sure to write as soon as I arrive. I expect the matter with my uncle will be resolved quickly, given the damning evidence against him," Gregory said.

"And Ebenezer?" Liana asked.

Gregory pressed his lips together in a grimace. "His punishment will not be as heavy as my uncle's, but he's likely to be confined in prison for a few years at least. He did try to kill Lady Emma, and her family will not overlook such an affront. But ..."

"But?" Dora questioned curiously.

"I intend to help him after he's served his time. He's a victim of my uncle, as strange as that sounds," Gregory responded. "He was born with little to his name, which made him susceptible to Lord Osborne's crafty designs. If I do not intervene by helping him, there's a good chance that his hatred will develop into something more dangerous."

"That's incredibly kind of you," Liana said, proud of the man she'd fallen in love with.

"Frankly, it's more of Russell's plan than mine. He's the sort of individual who likes to motivate and build up others."

Liana picked a tiny lint off his coat. "I can't wait to meet him."

He smiled and hugged her tightly. "You will very soon," he murmured in her ear. "When I return, I don't want us to wait another second before getting married."

"Does this mean we can go ahead and begin planning the wedding?" Alexander asked with a raised eyebrow.

"Yes. But only within the boundaries Liana expressed. She wants a small wedding."

"A small wedding," Dora repeated with a pained expression. "That's a rarely mentioned phrase in the Foxworth vocabulary, but we'll do what we can."

That drew bursts of laughter from everyone present, including the footmen who tried to hide their humor with sharp grunts. Gregory boarded the carriage, and, with a slight squeal, the vehicle sped away.

"While Gregory's gone, we can discuss the aspects of the wedding," Dora said, placing her arm across Liana's shoulders in a comforting gesture. "So don't dwell too much on his absence."

"I won't, or at least I'll try not to," Liana replied, leaning on her sister for support. "It feels absolutely wonderful to have everything return to normal."

"I'm glad to see you looking so happy," Alexander revealed, bumping her side affectionately with his arm. "I was always worried for you in those dark years when you were separated from Gregory."

"Truly?"

Alexander nodded. "You're my little sister, and I desire the best for you."

Liana blinked in confusion. "Then why didn't you interfere in any way to keep us together? I was under the impression that you wished to maintain a neutral air."

"I did try, but one can never be completely neutral in a matter involving one's sister and closest friend," her brother confessed with a slight lift of his shoulders. "I was the one who directly witnessed the sadness of both parties, after all."

He paused, and Liana turned to him, somehow knowing there was more.

"And what did you do about that?" she asked, knowing Alexander wasn't the sort to sit back and watch things happen helplessly.

"Don't tell Gregory this," he answered with a conspiratorial smile. "But I did receive the messages he'd sent to me in London, asking to discuss the new business idea. I ignored them and travelled down to Ravenmoore, in hopes that he'd travel here too and you two could meet again."

"It appears I'm not the only one prone to crafty plans," Dora observed wryly.

"Thank you," Liana told him, her soul brimming with gratitude. "If you hadn't done that, perhaps we'd still be stewing in the same tide of misery."

"On the contrary," Alexander said in a voice filled with certainty. "I have the feeling you two would have eventually found your way back to each other, interference or not."

Chapter Twenty-One

The special thing about London was the quick pace at which things typically happened. As soon as he arrived, Gregory visited the police quarters. There, he was informed that Lord Osborne was in custody and would remain so until the trials. Satisfied with the news, he moved on to his next point of visit.

St. James was an exclusive residential area where top aristocrats and other powerful individuals lived. It was also where Russell had built his home, a grand townhouse constructed in the architectural style of the Georgian period and with external walls a startling deep red and blue. It stood out from the surrounding houses by design, but the large iron-wrought gates dissuaded any ideas of an unwelcome visit.

During the scandal when he'd faced great condemnation until proven innocent, Gregory had watched helplessly as his vibrant brother faded into a shadow of his former self. It had seemed dangerous to leave Russell alone for a second, for fear that he would cause great harm to himself. He barely smiled, and at the rare times that he did, it was to manage a dark joke before going quiet again. Although it had hurt Gregory to witness his brother in such a state, he fully understood the reason for it. He, too, would be depressed if he'd been framed for murder and would shortly be facing the hangman's noose.

Love had saved Russell. Love in the form of Virginia Tabolt, a lady with bright red hair and an even brighter smile. An avid reader of mystery novels and the daughter of a Viscount, she'd taken up Russell's case and uncovered enough information to help him. The evidence that she gathered was sufficient for him to be pronounced innocent, resulting in a resounding welcome back into society.

Now they were happily married with two brilliant daughters, with Russell overseeing a lucrative career in merchant shipping.

As soon as Gregory's carriage rolled through the gates and he stepped out, he was pulled in by a strong pair of arms belonging to his brother. Whereas he'd been previously clean-shaven, Russell now sported a trimmed mustache, which suited him rather nicely.

"The past couple of days have been horrible for you, haven't they?" Russell said, fixing him with a pitying look as they drew apart. "It pains me that I could not be there with you."

"The letter I sent prior to traveling has reached you, then," Gregory responded. "If it helps, the terrible moments were brief, and I was rewarded afterwards with Lord Osborne's downfall."

Russell frowned. "A terrible man, that one. With any hope, we'll never have to deal with him again."

"We won't," Gregory said confidently. "Ebenezer's statement was effectively damning. That, coupled with the information from the police investigations and the investigator I hired, is enough to keep him locked away forever."

Russell grinned. "I wonder what's worse for Lord Osborne. Prison or a general scandal."

"The scandal, I presume. Knowing everyone will be made aware of what he's done will probably hurt him more than being confined."

"And a cousin named Ebenezer ..." Russell began, his face turning serious. "We will have to offer him our protection. He is worthy of a more fortunate existence."

Gregory nodded. The two men made their way into the house, with Russell talking nonstop about recent developments in London. A lady of the high court and a lord had been caught eloping to France. There were a few new investment opportunities to be alert to. A new club for accomplished gentlemen was in search of new members.

None were as intriguing as his thoughts about Liana. He felt a great yearning and longed to be back in her company, listening to the gentle sound of her voice.

"My beautiful lady has gone to the shops," Russell said proudly of his wife as they entered the high-ceilinged drawing room with distinctive French blue curtains. "She is the inspiration for my labors, after all. It would be a considerable misfortune to possess such wealth without a companion upon whom to bestow it."

Gregory chuckled in amusement. "And my nieces?"

"Out with their mother," Russell responded. "It's a rare thing to have the house so quiet, but I expect the noise will return before the day ends. You'll understand what I mean by dinnertime."

"I intend to depart for Ravenmoore in the evening. I'll return in time for the trial."

"Nonsense," Russell said. "Stay the night, at least. Or better still, remain in London until the trial is concluded."

Gregory opened his mouth to object, but Russell continued. "This is about that lady of yours, isn't it? Lady Liana?"

"Yes," Gregory replied, a smile leaping to his lips at the mention of her name. "Oddly, I had intended to remain in London until after the trial, but now I feel restless. I do not want to spend more days without her."

Russell glanced at him contemplatively. "Isn't she the same lady who broke your heart a while back?"

"Yes, but only because she wished for me to take up a good offer. Remember that trip to Brazil? I might have passed up on it if Liana hadn't pushed me to by ending our engagement."

"That's quite sacrificial of her," Russell said with a note of admiration. "Not many people would reject their loved one in a bid to push them toward success."

"But Liana did," Gregory said proudly. "And I'll always be indebted to her for that."

"She sounds like an incredible woman, and I look forward to meeting her."

"We'll be having the wedding soon, so you'll have that opportunity much earlier than you think."

Russell grinned. "You sound thoroughly lovestruck, which is a positive thing."

"I am," Gregory admitted, matching his brother's grin. "I absolutely am."

"So, you'll stay in London until the trial ends? Believe me, my wife, daughters, and I will ensure that you have a splendid time. After that, you can go home to your beloved Liana."

Gregory nodded. "That sounds like a good plan." *Soon.* He thought inwardly. Once this was all over, he'd be reunited with the woman he loved most in the world.

* * *

"It's a cong beetle," Dora said about the flying insect perched nearby on a sofa in the study.

"There's no such thing as cong beetles," Liana explained patiently, fiddling with the strings of her dulcimer. "However, there are other kinds of beetles, named for a variety of reasons."

"There may not be cong beetles, but I have decided to address this one as such," Dora declared with a twirl of her brush before returning her attention to her canvas.

The two sisters had found a way to combine their two favorite pastimes. Now they spent most afternoons in the study, with Dora painting as Liana played a melodious tune with the aid of her instrument.

"Cong beetle it is, or CB for short," Liana said in agreement, watching the insect with interest as it perched on another sofa. "It is said that the greatest people are those who leave their impact on the world, so you may be right in naming it yourself."

Dora nodded satisfactorily. "I'm glad you're beginning to familiarize yourself with my worldview."

"Similarly, it may also be egotistical—"

"No," Dora said, raising a hand in objection. "Frankly, I consider the first suggestion more appealing than the alternative."

"For good reason," Liana replied with a smile. "A bold individual is viewed more charitably than an egotist."

"Actually," said Dora, who had a fine appreciation for debates and arguments, "It is only a matter of how the situation is framed. In the right framing, an egotist may come out with more support than the bold individual."

"In what way?"

"An accomplished, wealthy gentleman who thinks too highly of himself would be well-received in his attempt to name an animal, in comparison to a bold pauper."

"That may be true, but in an ideal world, the bold pauper would be admired for showing such firmness of purpose."

Liana smiled to herself, thinking that Gregory would have quite a lot to contribute to the subject. He had studied at Eton, after all, and taken classes in ethics and philosophy. Not a day went by that she didn't think of him. Her tall, handsome man, who remained optimistic despite adversity.

The news of Lord Osborne's trial had spread like wildfire, and everyone in the countryside was talking about it. It was the main topic at Ravenmoore, which likely meant it was also the prevailing subject of discourse in London society. Liana was relieved to learn that Gregory's uncle had been found guilty of conspiracy and would be confined for the foreseeable future.

A few days had passed since the judgment, which meant Gregory would return soon. Liana had imagined their reunion repeatedly, but none of those thoughts would ever compare to the reality of him being present. He had written to her once since his departure, sharing how dearly he missed her and detailing his daily affairs.

She felt a combination of many emotions each time she thought of him—love, adoration, trust, and yearning. It was almost painful to count down the seconds until she could see him again.

Dora opened her mouth to say something, but her words were drowned out by sounds outside. Liana rushed to the window, where a familiar carriage with a team of healthy stallions had stopped at the manor's entrance. She held her breath as the door opened and a tall figure emerged, neatly dressed and his hair combed back.

Gregory was here! She'd barely registered the thought before her legs moved of their own free will—racing through the hallways and down the winding staircases. He turned fully toward her as she approached, barely stepping back as she rushed full force into his arms.

"You're here," she whispered into his suit, breathing in his comforting, masculine scent.

"I'm here," he said in agreement, running his hand through her hair with sweet affection. "Now and forever."

Epilogue

Liana and Gregory were wed at the start of autumn in a modest ceremony at which everyone they valued was in attendance. Alexander and Dora had managed to tread the fine line between their inner desire for a grand wedding and Liana's wishes for a small, intimate ceremony. The only guests present were those Liana and Gregory had personal relationships with. Similarly, the ceremony was held in a nearby chapel, a simple building that had stood on Ravenmoore land for many decades.

Gregory's brother, Russell, his gorgeous wife Victoria, and their two daughters had traveled from London to attend the wedding. Liana had been amused by Russell's friendly jokes and Victoria's attentiveness. A couple of businessmen who were also Gregory's good friends were present. They seemed kind, intelligent, and worldly in the same measure.

Liana didn't have too many friends, but her siblings and a few choice individuals were present to witness one of the happiest days of her life. It felt wonderful to meet everyone important to Gregory.

Similarly, it felt glorious to publicly declare what she had long believed in her heart. That she loved Gregory and intended to do so for eternity.

The air in the chapel was filled with anticipation as Liana and Gregory stood at the altar rail facing the clergyman. Her dress was snug and comfortable, precisely to her taste. It was an ivory silk dress with long, narrow sleeves and delicate embroidery at the hem. She had worked alongside a local seamstress to make the dress, which was an unconventional practice for an aristocratic lady. But Liana didn't care about anyone's murmurs or judgments. She'd always wanted to make her own wedding dress and was pleased to have that come to fruition.

Shyly, she glanced up at Gregory, a rush of intoxicating emotions drifting through her at the sight of him. He looked distinguished and handsome in his fine clothes, imported from France at Russell's insistence. A strand of dark hair curled along his forehead, refusing to be tamed. She kept her fingers steady at her side, resisting the urge to brush the lone strand affectionately into place.

There was a wide smile on Gregory's face, matching the one on hers. The air was thick with expectation as the vicar's brief sermon began. But for Liana, all voices melted away, leaving only Gregory. In a short while, he would become her husband. It was more than she could ever have hoped for.

On the vicar's urging, they turned to each other to exchange their vows. Liana's eyes brimmed with happy tears as Gregory declared that he would always love her in sickness, in health, and in all other circumstances. Beyond the words, the certainty in his eyes told her everything he'd just promised would be made a reality.

When it was Liana's turn, she recited her vows with an earnestness that evoked happy laughter from the guests. It was considered unfashionable for the groom and bride to be too affectionate in public with each other, but Gregory surprised everyone by kissing her briefly on the lips.

The guests erupted in loud applause and laughter, as the vicar blubbered in surprise. But all Liana could register was Gregory and the movement of his lips as his green eyes captured hers in a trance.

"I love you," she heard him say clearly through the applause.

"And I love you too, Gregory Holt," Liana responded with a smile so bright it matched the beauty of the sun.

The End.

Thank you for reading The Gentleman's Betrothal."

If you loved this book, you will love the first book of my Somersley Series Entitled "Governess Penelope and a Duke!"

It's a feel-good story about an unexpected second chance with a first love.

Click here and get your FREE copy of "The Governess and a Duke": https://dl.bookfunnel.com/a5l15u9hpa

In 1811 London, Penelope, a governess disowned by her father, discovers love while preparing her friend's niece for society.

This full-length second-chance romance offers a happily-ever-after ending,

Click here and get your FREE copy of Governess Penelope and a Duke now! https://dl.bookfunnel.com/a5l15u9hpa

Thank you for reading!
If you enjoyed this story, just a short review would mean so much. Your words help other readers find Liana and Gregory's journey.

https://www.amazon.com/review/create-review?&asin=B0FGHP6HZ4

Printed in Dunstable, United Kingdom